THE TANGLED WEB

Christopher Brown
The Tangled Web

All rights reserved
Copyright © 2025 by Christopher Brown

Published by Spines

ISBN: 979-8-89691-733-5

THE TANGLED WEB
SEQUEL TO "THE PLAYERS WEB"

CASRULE OXFORD

It didn't take Jazmyn and Devon too long to take to their New York way of life. Things were going so well Jazmyn stopped thinking about all the reasons she should have been leaving. She was feeling so content, she'd gotten comfortable with the way things were. She wasn't paranoid all the time about what might happen. She even started believing what Tango had told her a long time ago. He said if anything ever happened with the police, he'd make sure she and the kids were alright. Since she wasn't involved in anything illegal, the police couldn't do anything to her. If things got real bad with him and his business, Devon and she could go back to Virginia. He also made her promise to take little Monica back with her. It had taken long enough, but Jazmyn finally decided the best thing she could do was just relax. Why not take advantage of all the good things she had going on in her life? Devon was such a handful nobody at the school could handle him. He sure wasn't there to listen and learn. His attitude was so terrible, it was like he'd said to hell with school. Jazmyn couldn't get control of him no matter what she did. He was so out of control she figured he had to be going through some kind of phase. After a while, she gave up trying and just hoped he'd grow out of it one day. But it didn't look like he was interested in doing that.

As more time went by, he acted even worse in school. Jazmyn still hadn't told Tango that Devon was his son. She didn't see how that was going to do anybody any good. Why put even more pressure on a relationship that was hanging by a thread half the time? Tango had to be already tired of her nagging him about getting out of the business all the time. She didn't think telling him Devon was his kid would encourage him to get out of his smooth criminal lifestyle. The way Devon acted in school, she doubted if he'd think that was such a good deal. Besides, she didn't see any reason to rock the boat. She loved getting away from her apartment and going up to Tango's. They had some good times being alone together. That was their own private space. She spent a lot of her time on the top floor with him. They managed to get into a few deep and intimate conversations sometimes. It was those conversations that made her feel a really deep connection with him. They made her feel like he knew more about her and what went on in her mind than anyone had before. Tango had shown her new things about her body and given her feelings she'd never had with anyone before. She had to laugh at herself when she thought about her romantic experience. In her whole life, she'd only been to bed with three guys, and Tango was one of them. Even she had to admit that was pretty pitiful. Anyway, all that really mattered was that she was happy. So what if it wasn't the kind of life she'd pictured for herself? When she stopped and looked at it for what it was, she still had to smile. She smiled because she never would have imagined she could feel like this for him again.

Here she was with a good, loyal man, that kept the cash flow coming in who'd do anything she asked him to. On top of that, he made sure her badass son was safe. Devon was somewhere she didn't have to worry about anybody doing anything to him. Plus, his badass was happy. If he wasn't somewhere doing who knows what with Monica, he was raising hell with a bunch of the kids on the block. As much as she tried to find fault, she couldn't deny that they were happy. There wasn't anything Devon wanted he couldn't have gotten if he'd just acted like he had some sense. If he behaved in school he could have had more than he dreamed of. Well, so far, everybody's pockets were safe from that happening. It could be a beautiful life if she would let herself live it. But she couldn't stop tracing every little thing all the way down the line. There wasn't much for Jazmyn to do while everybody else was busy carrying on with their lives of crime. That's why she went up to Tango's apartment and waited for him. That's the only escape she enjoyed from the boredom that always seemed to be trying to swallow her up. Sometimes, Jazmyn got completely naked in the middle of the day and paraded around Tango while he was trying to work. She loved messing up his busy schedule. No matter how hard he tried to stay focused, he'd still end up breaking down and letting her take him into her mouth. That's when she showed him she was the one who could give him all the attention he deserved. When she did that, he took her body over and made her feel like she belonged to him in every way. She loved to use her mouth because it drove him crazy. When he was taken like that, he stretched her body and used it for his pleasure. That was all she really needed from him to be happy. When she had him like that, she knew he would always be hers.

Public school #168 was where Devon first met Keith "Money" Hampton. At the time, they didn't know they'd become the best of friends. All they knew was that they didn't like school. Since they were stuck in the same homeroom, they soon discovered they liked the same kinds of trouble. They got their troublemaking day started bright and early on the way to school. After a little practice, they became experts at bum-rushing the magazine stands on the street. Devon had Keith distract the vendors by acting like he was stealing. Then, while their attention was on him, Devon stuffed as many magazines and newspapers in his book bag as he could. After that, they hustled off everything on the train for half price. Everybody on the train was headed into work in Manhattan, so they had a captive audience. They did that before they ever got to school. Sometimes, they missed the opening bell for class, and they'd have to spend the first half of the school day on the street. Then, they would wait until lunchtime, that way, nobody would notice them sneaking back into the school. Once they got back in the school, they headed for the cafeteria. They'd get some food and wait until lunch period was over. Then, they'd merge back in with the rest of the cattle on the way to their next class. It might have been a coincidence, but they had pretty much the same grades. Yeah, they were the same, bad. They cheated by taking the other kids' papers whenever they took tests. If any of them gave them any problems, they threatened them. As soon as word got around, the smart kids all knew what they had to do. They'd give up their test papers without even being asked for it. The teachers passed them to get rid of them because it sure wasn't scholarship that got them into high school. It was equal parts luck, nerve, and too large of a class size that did it. None of the teachers in high school thought they'd get their diploma, and it turns out they were right. After two years, the high school decided they'd seen enough. They were over the age limit and couldn't be forced to go to school. The principal told them not to even come back. They'd been waiting for them to turn seventeen anyway. After that, they didn't have to deal with them anymore. According to the law, after the age of 17, a school isn't required to force you to attend. That was right up their alley, now they were free to do whatever they wanted.

They were so happy they hardly knew where to start. They had so many ideas they couldn't decide which one they wanted to do first. The one thing they knew was they wanted to get their hands on cash by any means necessary. They started out working the train stations. There was always a steady supply of new and different victims coming through there. First, they had to perfect their game. Once they got it together, nobody was safe. But those train station hustles got old fast. The transit cops started recognizing them on sight, and that was not good for business. They had to move on after that. Then, they started trying out their skills on the street. They went from snatching purses and grabbing gold chains to trying to be pickpockets. They even gave strong armed robbery a try, but finding the right victim was too hard. If you happened to come through the train station when they were in there, it's a good bet you wouldn't make it back home with everything you left with. The money wasn't big enough fast enough for Devon. They kept trying for a few months, but by the end of the year, they were selling slum jewelry and running three card molly games. Devon was always the hungry one. Always trying to have the most and best of everything. He wanted to be living the life of a big-time hustler, but he was too impatient. Devon never wanted to listen to anybody else. He didn't care about the risks if he thought the payoff was big enough. He'd grown up idolizing Tango. Ever since he came to New York, he'd been watching the way Tango ran his program. It was only natural that he'd want to be like him one day. He admired Tango and how he moved. Not just because he was a big-time player and hustler; that's not what mattered to him. He cared about how Tango was always in control of everything. Tango never got too excited about anything. He was always wearing the freshest jewelry, had the freshest clothes and only drove the nicest cars. What Devon loved more than all that was Tango always had stacks of cash. That's what Devon really craved.

Devon's dreams were full of desires and wishes bigger than everybody else's. He felt his life was standing still. In his head, he was going nowhere fast, but everybody else was rising up over him. The more ambitious he became, the more reckless he got. He took way more chances than he should have, but that nothing could slow him down. When he got older, he and Keith started hustling like grownups in the street. Then one day, Keith came up and told Devon, "Hey man, I ain't feeling this stick-up shit no more. You know, I wasn't never really down with it in the first place." Devon wasn't surprised. He had noticed how Keith was always acting scary when it was time to put in some work. "Man, I don't know why you waited until the last minute to say something, you know I can't do this shit by myself. Just get down with me on a few more jobs until I can find somebody else to get down with." Devon could tell by the look on his face he wasn't going to do it. "Look, dude, I did all I'm trying to do of that shit. The real money is in the dope game. If you keep playing Russian roulette with these stickups, one of these days, you're gonna come up snake eyes." Devon wasn't trying to hear none of that, he waved his hand in his face. "Nigga, you ain't complain when you was counting them stacks though, right? Now that you're playing stupid games with them crackheads and hypes, you want to roll up like a bitch on me. That's alright, don't come back when your money get funny."

He cut Keith back when he started going so hard in the drug game. That was when he really fell off. Keith was chasing after every lick and hanging around some of the nastiest females in the hood. It was like he wouldn't or couldn't stop himself. When Devon saw how hard he was stuck in the dope game he knew he had to step off. Keith started off selling weed and some hash, but before long, he moved up to PCP. In no time, he was mixing that with acid and speed. He was having a lot of fun and making a lot of cash, but he wasn't satisfied. He wanted to be big in the cocaine game. That was right around the time the crack craze hit. When that went down, he was right where he wanted to be. He got turned out by the hustle. He was too worried about what the fiends wanted. There was always a bunch of hypes somewhere around. If they needed to find him, he made sure they didn't have to look too hard. Drugs had them all hypnotized. Everybody was always trying to catch a feeling. If it would fit into a package, Keith would sell it.

Devon wasn't built like that. He wasn't going to depend on anybody else to make his money. He tried to roll with the drug hustle for a minute but ended up saying to hell with that. He started hanging around the pool room with some of the thugs he knew from the hood. Devon wanted then to put him down on something. That was the best way he could figure out to be included with their crew. Whenever they were in there, Devon would get close to them. He used to hang out in there when he didn't make it to school, so they all knew him. They were in there so much they looked like furniture. They'd sit around on the tables in the back, talking shit and trading lies. Old-ass Donnie was in charge of the pool room, but he didn't care about them being there as long as they kept the noise down. He figured it was better for business if the place looked busy. Nobody wanted to come and spend money in an empty spot. Devon came in to try and get in their mix. Chucky had to start some shit with him first. "Yo little nigga, how come you ain't got your ass in a school somewhere?" Devon rolled his eyes with an attitude. "The same reason you ain't got your ass in one. They ain't paying niggas to carry books around and listen to a bunch of bullshit. What they're talking about in there ain't gonna put no money in my pockets."

Chucky wasn't going for none of that smart shit from him, "Oh, so you're too smart to go to school? What do your broke ass know about getting money?" Devon had to let him know he wasn't going for it. "I know we're both up in here, if I don't know shit, you can't know too much more than me." Everybody cracked up except Snake. He wasn't laughing because he'd just thought of something. While they were going back and forth, something clicked in his head. "Damn, Chuck, the little nigga told your old ass what time it was." Chucky didn't want to hear it, so he tried to go in on Snake. "He ain't telling me shit I ain't know already. A nigga got to know things before he can do things. When it comes to getting money, I already know what to do." Snake didn't wasn't trying to hear that. He'd heard all of Chucky's excuses more than once. He'd been hearing them for as long as he'd known him. Snake just shook his head and gave him a sly look. "Don't forget, a little nigga like him can be useful when you want to throw a fool off guard, ya nigh mean?"

This time, when they looked at each other, their minds clicked on the same thing. Chucky and Snake quickly got up and went in the bathroom. Devon would be the perfect distraction. They'd been planning to rob an Arabian store that was about to open. They'd already cased it out and were almost ready to do it. They just didn't want anybody in their crew to be in on it. After a few minutes in the bathroom, Snake and Chucky came right up to Devon. Snake started talking first. "Listen up, little nigga, I like your swag. But how do we know you can put in work with us? If you ain't the scary type, we might give you a chance to prove yourself. But first, you've got to show us what we want to see. If you're really about that life, we might let you be down. That's the only way you can get paid like us." Devon was down, but he wasn't going to be nobody's flunky. He knew if he didn't watch out, they'd have him sitting in a jail cell.

Devon was talking to Snake but looking at Chucky. "Yeah, well, you don't have to worry about me, I know how to handle my business. All I want is to get paid like I'm supposed to be. I'm not trying to get caught up in no bullshit that ain't worth shit." Chucky spoke up then. "Yo nigga, if I'm getting down on with it, the cash is real. If you're trying to get paid, you'd be a fool not to be down with us. When you work with us, you're guaranteed to get paid."

Snake could tell Devon was hungry to hit a lick. That's what made it easy to catch a nigga slipping. When they're thirsty, you can catch them moving fast and thinking slow. The old heads used to call it speedballing. That's what Snake and Chucky were letting Devon do to himself. They needed a frontman and didn't want none of their boys to be the first one in or the last man out. Going in first was the most dangerous part. You didn't know what you'd be running into. Devon was skeptical, but he wanted to let them know what time it was.

"Yo check it, I'm letting ya'll know, I ain't no sucker in this shit. I'm down for whatever, but trust me, I want all of mine just like you want all of yours." Chucky didn't like the way that sounded. It sounded like Devon was questioning their integrity. "You must not know who you're dealing with, do you? We couldn't stay in business if we was fucking over our partners. Just make sure you do what you're supposed to do. When you prove you can do your job, we'll show you how good it is to be down with us." Devon just smirked and rolled his eyes. "Yeah well, we'll see about all that after this shit is done." Chucky and Snake walked outside with Devon to tell him what he had to do. They got their plan together, and agreed to meet on the street first thing in the morning.

The next morning, at 7:30 am, Devon was standing on the corner of Forrest and Garvey. He could see Chucky and Snake down at the corner on the other side of the street. They were waiting for him to go up the alley to the back door. When they saw that, they'd start walking down the street. Devon made sure his stocking mask wasn't showing. He pushed more of it up in the UPS cap before pushing the buzzer. A voice upstairs said, "Yeah! Who is it?" In a clear voice with a little extra bass. "UPS delivery." His hurried heartbeat mixed in his ears with the sound of footsteps on the stairs. He pulled the stocking mask down all the way over his chin and blocked the peephole with the UPS emblem on the hat. As soon as he saw the door start to open, he pushed his whole weight against it. The guy fell on his back against the stairs and Devon quickly pushed the barrel of his 38 Special in the man's frightened face. In an authoritarian tone, he said, "Shut up and turn over." while pulling roughly on the man's shoulder. He flipped him over and said, "Now, lay your ass still right there before I have to put a bullet in you." He turned the UPS cap around so he could see what he was doing. The stocking mask was making it a little harder to breathe. There was so much adrenaline pumping through his body he didn't care about breathing right then. It felt like his body was full of electricity as he impatiently waited for Chucky and Snake.

It felt like it had taken them forever, but they came in with their masks pulled down. Snake said, "Alright, keep him right here, we'll go upstairs and get the loot." Devon said, "What am

I staying down here for? I'm coming up, too." Snake was already up the stairs, and Chucky wasn't about to argue. He just said, "Whatever." and made his way up the stairs. Devon grabbed the owner by his belt and pushed him up the stairs in front of him. Once upstairs, he pushed the frightened man into one of the empty rooms. While Chucky and Snake were going through everything, looking for money and valuables, Devon pushed the man face down on the floor. "Stay right there, and don't move." Then Devon took out two pieces of rope and hung them around his neck. While Chucky and Snake frantically searched for loot, he tied the man's ankles to his wrists from behind. Next he put a loop in the other rope and put that around the man's neck. He tied the end of the rope around his neck to the one tied to his ankles. If he struggled or tried to move, the rope on his neck would tighten up and cut off his air. Devon watched them looking everywhere for money, and got close to the owner's ear. "You'd better tell me what I want to know, or I'll just have to kill your ass and call this a big waste of time. Where did you hide the money? I'm not asking you again."

The man was stubborn, but Devon could see he was terrified. He wasn't going to be an easy one to scare, but when Devon cocked the gun right next to his ear, he gave in. "There isn't much money here, I was just getting ready to open the store up." Devon put the barrel in his face and said, "I'm only giving you one more chance to tell me what I want to know. After that, I'm going to put a gag in your mouth and start breaking fingers." The look on the man's face showed his resolve evaporating. Quietly, he told Devon, "It's in the floorboards at the back of the store. Please don't kill me, I have a family. I just want to make it back home." Devon told him, "You can go home after I get this money." He tore off the man's shirt sleeve and stuffed it in his mouth for a gag before he went up front. Devon was tired of watching them search. "Yo, what are ya'll doing up here! What's the problem? Ain't nobody trying to be up in here all day." He could see Snake was pissed off and ready to get out of there too. "Man, don't worry about what's going on with us, we've got this bag of cash and are about to bounce. Just make sure his ass is tied up good, and we'll meet back up with you in a few." Devon looked at how everything was torn up and scattered before he said, "So ya'll just going to leave me in here? Who's going to watch the door for me?" Snake did not feel like hearing that shit, and he wasn't about to be giving out no explanations either. "Look, little nigga, get your ass out of here the same way you got in." He grabbed Chucky by the collar and said, "Let's go."

As soon as they left, Devon went to where the owner said the money was. He looked all around and didn't see any hiding places on the floor. He went back to the owner and said, "Alright, I'm not asking you any more questions, if you lie to me this time, it's gonna be your last chance to tell the truth." The man shook his head and said, "I swear it's back there on the floor." All while trying to keep the tension out of the rope around his neck. Devon went back and started looking again. He looked for any empty spaces or loose floorboards. He still didn't see where a safe could be. Then he noticed some boards under a work table were kind of uneven. There were a few gaps in them, so he got a screwdriver and got down on his hands and knees to pry them apart. He got the first one up, and then the rest of them came up. He pushed them aside and saw a blue bank pouch. He pulled it out and unzipped it. Inside, it had stacks of 100-dollar bills. He quickly leafed through the bills and estimated it to be about fifteen thousand dollars. He laughed because of the money but was more happy because he didn't have to share with those two idiots. Devon went over to the man on the floor and said, "Look, man, I'm leaving you breathing, that's a good deal for you. Just don't forget, when the police start asking you a lot of questions, you can't remember a damn thing. I'll cut this rope from around your neck so you can breathe easier. Just don't give me no reason to come back here and hurt whoever I find." Devon cut the rope so the man could relax and breathe, then stuffed the pouch and pistol down in the back of his pants. Going down the stairs, he couldn't help thinking, this was a beautiful day in the neighborhood.

Devon stopped at the bottom of the stairs and took a second to get his mind together. He snatched the stocking mask off before going out the side door, then stuck the UPS cap in his back pocket. He walked down the street, making sure his shirt covered up the bag of loot and his ratchet. His mind was going some of everywhere, but the main thing on it was getting off the street. He had to get the loot and gun from the robbery off of him. The only place he could stash it was back at the building. He had to sneak in because everybody thought he was still going to school. It was almost 8:30 by now, if his moms saw him, she'd give him hell. She stayed on his ass for not doing something he was supposed to do. He didn't know what he'd say if she asked him why he wasn't in school. He crept in the front door and headed straight for the basement. So far, nobody had seen him. He crept down the stairs and prayed nobody came down there. After looking all around, he found a good spot in the boiler room. He fit every-thing behind the compartment for the blower motor on the furnace. After that, he headed back up the stairs to get a change of clothes. He didn't want to be walking around in the same clothes he'd just pulled a robbery in. He had to take a chance and go back home. He took a deep breath and knocked on the door. When nobody came, he hurried up and went inside. This early in the morning, his mom was probably at Tango's. That worked out perfectly for him. He quickly changed into some fresh gear and got out of there as fast as he could.

Devon hurried back to meet Chucky and Snake in the pool room. He wanted to see how much his cut was and if they had any other jobs lined up. It was only 9:30, so it was still too early for many people to be in there. Like always, they were in the back, looking suspicious. Devon decided to give them some drama first. "Yo, why ya'll niggas leave me by myself like that? What if I needed help or something? Ya'll ain't know if the po po was on their way or not! Snake just looked at him. "Yeah, then all of us could have got caught in there right? We left because the job was over, you stayed because your job was to tie his ass down." Then speaking like a baby tone he said, "What happened? Was you scared in there all by yourself?" Of course, Chucky had to say something too. "I guess you thought it would look pretty normal for a whole crowd of motherfuckers to be seen leaving from up out of a crime scene huh?" Devon still wasn't ready to let it go. "Man fuck that noise, all I know is that was cold shit to do. That shit ain't right, I wouldn't have done ya'll like that. Just give me my cut. How much was in that bag anyway?" Chucky said, "Man it wasn't but $850 dollars in the bag. We all get $250 apiece."

Devon rolled his eyes and said, "What? You trying to tell me that's all the money that was up in there? Man that ain't shit for three grown ass niggas to be splitting. I did the most work so I should get the $350. Ya'll two can split that $500 that's left." Devon didn't care for school but he could count up some money real quick and correct. They looked at each other like messing with him had been a bad idea. They wasn't about to humor his ass. Snake just stared at him. "Listen fool, you knew what it was when you went in there. It is what it is and that's all it's ever going to be. Take your cut and count it up as more than you had before we told you what was up." Devon couldn't do anything but smirk and chalk it up. "Yeah alright. Ya'll got me this time. But next time I'll be the one making the split." He took the money from Snakes hand but never stopped complaining. "That still ain't how you treat people that's down with you, you know? I wouldn't have done ya'll like that." Inside, he was gloating over the cash he'd stashed away.

Devon started doing robberies by himself after that. At least once a month he pulled his ratchet on some fool. Nobody knew he'd been thrown out of school, so he kept getting up in the morning and leaving like normal. With all the free time on his hands, he stayed looking for new ways to get paid. The pool room and the New York streets were his classrooms. Jazmyn was bored all the time. She was always looking for some way to keep herself busy. She wanted to do something to help Tango, and stay in his face all the time too. She showed him how the computer software they used at the real estate office could be used in his business. She taught him how to use it for book keeping and keeping track of all of his loan accounts. After he started using his computer like a file cabinet, he became a real detail freak. Tango saw that it saved him a lot of money and time. Jazmyn made sure to show him all the ways he could put that extra time to good use.

Time was the only thing she needed when she was bored.

Hanging around his office she never knew when she might get a chance to pull his dick out. After she finished sucking it and rubbing it all over her face, nothing could keep her from climbing up on it and riding until they were both satisfied. He complained about her wasting his time, but she knew he was lying. He loved it when she interrupted him like that. Besides, she was just making herself useful. One day, when she was sitting around in his office waiting for him to come in, she started to feel her eyelids getting heavy. Since Devon wouldn't be home for a few hours, she decided to catch a quick cat nap. She slipped off her shoes and curled up on his big velvet covered couch. As she was trying to get comfortable, she snuggled down into the thick cushions and something hard stuck her in her butt. Aggravated at her nap being ruined, she scooted up and stuck her hand in the couch to see what it was. When she reached down there, she got out a cell phone. The screen had a bunch of missed calls on it from an area code she didn't know. Puzzled, she told herself she'd give it to Tango when he came back, and threw it in her purse.

It seemed like she was only asleep for few minutes when Tango's voice woke her up. Of course it was his big, loud, and inconsiderate self coming in. She stood up and tried to quickly get her hair back in place. Smoothing the wrinkles out of her skirt, she sat back down trying to look like she'd been awake. He was so engrossed in his phone conversation he didn't pay her or how she was looking any attention. Whoever he was talking it must have been important. The look on his face was intense, and he definitely wasn't happy about whatever he was hearing. When he noticed her sitting there, he shot her a quick smile, but that's all. He quickly turned his attention back to his conversation. He lowered his tone when he went out of the office, but Jazmyn knew something wasn't right. A few minutes later he got off the phone and came over to show her some love. His hugs and kisses felt disconnected and brittle to her. Jazmyn felt the difference and wanted to know what was wrong. "What's going on baby? Can I do something to make it better?" He didn't have to say anything, his look told her he was tense and resigned to whatever was happening. "I wish there was something you could do baby doll, but I would never involve you in this. Don't worry though, everything will work itself out for the best. As long as I've got you, I've got everything I need." Seeing her brown eyes sparkle, and her beautiful smile, did make him feel a little better.

He needed something to help him forget the bad news his Columbian connect just gave him. He needed to enjoy living and give himself a good time. That was something he still wanted do, for a little while anyway. What was going on in Columbia, with the State department getting into the drug business, wasn't something he could do anything about. Instead of stressing over it, he wrapped Jazmyn in his arms and held her close. This time the feeling she got made her juices simmer. Showing her how he felt about her meant more than whatever words he could say. This is why she knew all she needed to know about his love. The feelings she felt were good, and she knew she never wanted to be without him again. When she felt his touch it made her feel things inside she'd only known with him. In her heart she felt like he was hers again. She was loving life so much she forgot all about the phone she found. She almost forgot Devon would be coming home hungry around four o clock. She would have to cut her time with Tango short. Her normal duties of mother and parole officer were calling. She silently cursed the clock and made her way down the stairs. She didn't have that much time to fix dinner, whatever it was would have to be fast. The refrigerator said baked chicken and mixed vegetables. That's all she had time to make. If she threw in a few baked sweet potatoes and dinner rolls, Devon's greedy ass would devour it.

As she was hurrying to get the food ready, Jazmyn kept hearing a weird buzzing sound. It was somewhere in the house, but she didn't have time to see where it was coming from. It took her three trips around the house before she zeroed in on her purse. She'd forgotten all about the phone from Tango's couch! The vibration was somebody from the 904 blowing it up. She still didn't know where the 904 was, but she knew an easy way to find out. She gave in to her curiosity and answered in her most professional voice. "Yes? Who would you like to speak with?" The response she got was so vulgar it shocked her, "Don be tryna' play dat bull shit on me nah woman. Ya know me got a lot of danger in me heart fa ya now. Ya keep playin dese games an ya gwana make me crush ya lak a bug." They obviously didn't know who they were talking to, but the accent they spoke with made her want to keep the charade up, "You don't have to talk like that to me, just tell me who you want to speak to and I'll do what I can to help." That must have made him mad because the voice got even louder. "Yah say yah gwana do wat yah can? Beech you gwana do more dan dat. Ya gwana do wat I tells ya ta do. Ya betta leesen ta me Ellie, ya owes us evathang ya gat, an ya gwana make up fa da way dat stick up went down on da beach. Dats wat me know! Ya know da way it wen down was fucked up! Dat was me brothas an ma fatha what got kilt. Ya owe dis crew an dats a debt yah gwana pay beech. We gon take erythin from dat bumma clod Tanga. Him numba and dope cash gwana be ours. His ass gon be da inntres on ya debt if he be tryna stop us. We been waitin fa 13 years ta git what yah owe an we ain gwan be waitin no mo. Wen we come up dere ta New Yok ya gwana give us ereythang ya know bout. Wen we git dat we gwana leev ya breevin. Ya unnerstand me words beech?"

When she heard Tango's name her heart froze. She didn't know what to do from there, but the danger and fear she felt were too real to ignore.

Tango's life was in some kind of danger because of something Ellie had done. Something had to be done about it, and it looked like it was going to be her. Jazmyn felt trapped. She was being pulled into their world of treachery and violence. She didn't know what could happen to Tango or herself if she got involved. But she was in it now, and didn't see how she could get back out. She wanted to tell Tango about the phone call and what she'd heard, but she didn't want to lay even more on him. She didn't really even know what was going on. If she confronted Ellie about it she could find out what she knew about the people making these threats. Who was this mysterious Jamaican, and why was he so angry with her? She needed to figure things out, but now she had to keep the game going. "I've got to hang up now, but I'll call you back soon." Then she shut off the phone.

Her heart was pounding so hard she could feel it in her temples. They had said Ellie's name, so they must have thought they were talking to her. Jazmyn didn't know what it all meant, but she wanted to know what happened in Florida 13 years ago. Why had people died because of it?. She was too shook up to think straight, somebody had to do something. There was no time to waste, but what she needed more than anything right then was a stiff drink! At that moment Devon came through the door. Before he'd even gotten in the door good, he came at her with another of his almost daily complaints. "Mama, how long am I supposed to walk around watching everybody else drive by me? I need a car so I can get to where I'm trying to go, you know?" Jazmyn gave him her sternest look and said, "Listen to me boy, don't come in here talking that nonsense to me. The only place you're trying to go is to jail. That's the only place you're headed to if you keep running around here with that Keith Hampton character. If you want to end up there, you've already got a good head start. I hope you don't think nobody knows he's pushing dope around here. If you do, you're about as smart as he is. Those jail birds you hang around with down at that pool room ain't no step up either. I already told you, I'm not doing anything until you show me how much you want me to do it. So far all you want me to do is to let you learn the hard way." Devon wasn't getting anywhere with her, so he let out an exasperated sigh and sped off to his room. As soon as he got inside he locked the door and took out the sneaker box he kept in the back of his closet. He opened it and looked at the neatly arranged stacks of cash inside. He couldn't help counting up the stacks again. They were arranged in stacks of a thousand each, with a rubber band around each stack. He didn't care what anybody said, he was getting a car of his own. His only problem would be explaining where he got the money from.

Jazmyn was still thinking about that phone call. It was going to drive her crazy until she found out what happened in Florida. Monica had been a baby back then, she wasn't going to be any help. The only one she could ask was Mike. He was old enough to remember what happened before they got here. She wasn't worried about him saying anything to Ellie, she could tell he didn't like her ass either. While Devon stuffed his face in the dining room, Jazmyn got on her laptop and went to the real estate office website. Every now and then she liked to look at the sales and listings to check out what was happening down there. The business had been doing very well since she left and there was a lot of new construction going on. A lot of the small towns around Richmond were expanding at a breakneck pace. That meant a lot of new people were looking to upgrade their housing situation. That meant the real estate business was bound to get even better. She still hadn't become a licensed broker in the city yet. Breaking into a brand new market without having your own office was tough. She wasn't about to work in somebody else's office and help them get rich. She had a company of her own in Virginia that was turning money over very well. Truth is, she was waiting for Tango to make good on all of his promises. He told her a long time ago he'd leave his criminal life behind, so now all she had to do was live that long. She didn't have time to worry about what Tango wasn't doing, Ellie needed to be dealt with, and the longer it took to get to the bottom of it, the closer the trouble was to New York. She needed Monica to tell Mike she wanted to talk to him. Maybe then she'd find out how much he knew.

Jazmyn had a battle plan, now she had to put it into action. Ellie lived on the second floor like her so she walked down the hall and knocked on her door. Ellie asked "Who is it?" Jazmyn tried to sound friendly and cheerful when she said, "Oh hey Ellie, it's Jazz I'm just looking for Monica," The door opened and as Ellie was walking away she said, "Come on in Jazmyn, she should be back in a few minutes. She just ran down to the pawn shop on the corner. She just had to get some of them old big ass earrings she saw in there." Jazmyn shot her a cheap smile and said, "Hey, at least she saves her money." Ellie went on cleaning the pots in the sink as she talked, "Monica's got a lot to learn about a lot of things, but she damn sure knows how to squeeze her some money." Her tone had Jazmyn feeling like it was time to end their girl time moment. "That's good, because I'm trying to see if she wants to make this money I've got for her. I need her to clean out my refrigerator and straighten some of my cabinets out. I can't be getting down on my hands and knees no more. She's the right age to be doing all that hands and knees stuff." Then with a slight laugh said, "When she gets back tell her I'm waiting for her alright?" "Oh I'll definitely let her know about getting some more money. Trust me, she'll run down there to make that money with the quickness." Jazmyn turned to leave and said, "Alright, I'm going down there to try and make some progress on the rest of the cleanup." "Okay Jaz, take it easy."

When Jazmyn got back Devon was gone. Of course his plate was still right where he left it. She didn't have time to worry about how sloppy her son was, she had bigger fish to fry. Jazmyn tried again to get into the banking app on her laptop. She wanted to transfer a deposit from her company account into her personal account. But when she put in the password, the laptop didn't recognize it. She was about to get pissed when there was a soft knock on the door. She was aggravated about the password but calmed down enough to say "Who is it?" Monica said, "It's me Miss Jazz, aunt Ellie said you wanted me to do some work for you?" Jazmyn smiled when she opened the door. She really was tickled when she saw all the supplies Monica had. "You weren't playing about making this money were you?" Monica had a bucket of sponges and a bunch of spray cleaning products in both hands. "Hey Miss Jazz, you can't go to work if you don't have the tools you need. Ellie said you'd pay me to clean, so I figured the better I clean, the more money I'd make." Jazmyn closed the door behind her, still shaking her head. The easy way she smiled always gave Jazmyn a warm feeling. Monica left her supplies sitting by the door, and that was right about where Jazmyn expected them to stay. She had to smile at how serious this girl was about handling her business. She couldn't understand why that devil of hers didn't get the same prescription in his system. "Come on in here and talk with me for a minute Monica, I've got some stuff I want to ask you about." Monica had a puzzled look on her face as she followed her to the table to sit down. "Hey Miss Jazz, if you want to know about anything I know, I'll make sure you know it too." "Moni, I need to know about something that happened when you were still a little kid. Did anything bad happen in Florida before you and Mike came to New York? I know you were little, but do you remember anything about it?"

As soon as she heard the question a strange look came over her face. The look told Jazmyn a lot. She knew it had to be something really traumatic to affect her like that after so much time had passed. Whatever went on had affected her personality and was still upsetting to her. Usually when Monica talked, she moved her hands and smiled a lot. But this time she wasn't doing any of that. All of a sudden she was quiet, this personality change was shocking to Jazmyn. Monica's eyes were cast down as she sat there almost squirming in her seat. "Dang, Miss Jazz it's crazy you asking me about that. When me and Mike came here it wasn't like it was by choice. We *had* to come here because my mom and dad got killed. We had to come live with aunt Ellie because we didn't have anybody down there to take care of us. Mike knows all about what happened, but all I know is they got killed by some Jamaicans who was robbing them. Mike told aunt Ellie what happened and she made us come up here. Now since he's grown, Mike thinks he can go back and get them for what they did. He keeps saying he's gonna get them niggas. But Miss Jazz, ain't nothing going to bring my mom and dad back." Jazmyn took her hand and lovingly squeezed it. Monica thought to herself, "If I could have another mom I'd love if it was Jazmyn." Jazmyn could see how their talk was bothering her. "Baby, you don't have to talk about this anymore. I know it's making you feel bad. It's hard to go over stuff like this, so now we'll just let it go alright?" Monica's head bobbed up and down. "I do want you to do something for me though, if you can." Monica nodded her head and said, "I told you, anything you want me to do for you is good as done." "Well this is easy, just tell Mike I want to talk to him. Tell him it's better if we don't meet around here." Jazmyn handed her a piece of paper with her number on it and said, "When he calls me we'll get together somewhere else, ok?" Monica's face brightened up then. "Oh you know that's not a problem Miss Jazz, I'll tell him as soon as I see him. I'll give him your number and then ya'll can hook up ok?"

Jazmyn couldn't help smiling when she looked at Monica. She was more than just smart, the girl always had something going on in her mind. "Baby, I wish you'd give that devil Devon some of your brain power. He's so busy trying to act smart he can't do the things smart people do." Monica couldn't help but smile. "I know that's right Miss Jazz, you can't see it but he is trying. He just thinks he's supposed to be the boss of everything. He thinks he can run everything but he never wants to listen to anybody. If he listened sometime maybe he could learn what he don't know. I try to tell him things but he won't listen to me. He tells me I ain't nothing but a dumb broad, cause you know, he's such a big man. Hear him tell it, I ain't nothing but a kid." Jazmyn just shook her head. "If you're a kid he must be a damn toddler. You're the one that's in here talking to me, trying to help me out. I'll bet you he's somewhere right now trying to get into some kind of trouble." Monica's face softened a little. "He's just got to grow up some that's all. When he gets himself together he'll be alright. Until then he's going to be a handful." Jazmyn felt like she needed to take a look at this girl's birth certificate. She was way too smart to be just sixteen. Jazmyn knew she had to let her go back home, she'd been down there too long to just be cleaning. "As long as he's got you on his side he'll be ahead of the game. I just wonder how long it's going to take before you get tired of his mess." Monica's eyes rolled up in her head when she smiled and said, "Oh don't worry about that Miss Jazz, he can't shake me off his ass, oops my bad. I don't quit on nothing when I know it's worth the trouble." Monica was going to be a beautiful young woman one day. "Devon better snatch you up before he goes trying to run the world. You're just what he needs if he wants to get ahead." Monica smiled shyly and said, "Awwww you're supposed to say that kind of stuff Miss Jazz. I just hope he knows the difference between somebody being in his corner and somebody just being on your corner." Jazmyn pressed a crisp $100 bill in her hand and winked at her. "Thanks for doing all this hard work baby. You did a real good job on my refrigerator and cabinets, okay? Tell your aunt Ellie thanks for sending you down to do this work for me alright?" Monica picked up the supplies with a puzzled look on her face. "Why are you telling me that. We didn't clean anything?" Then she smiled when she caught on and said, "Okay, I'll make sure I tell her it wasn't that much work to do. It was just kind of hard getting up in all the corners." Then with a wink and a smile she headed back down the hall.

The afternoon traffic was just another thing getting on Jazmyn's nerves today. She hated to navigate the obstacles and insanity of New York city traffic during rush hour. There was a million other things she could be aggravated about, this traffic didn't have to be the one that pushed her over the edge. She was still trying to figure out how to get around what was keeping her from getting a realtors license in New York city. The real estate game was different than in Virginia. Her family owned the office, so all she had to do was pass the test and she was automatically certified. She was showing properties and making sales the next day. In the city it wasn't that simple. It was more about who you knew and who owed you. In other words, if you didn't have some kind of inside connection or somebody pulling strings for you in the real estate game, you weren't going to catch a break on any good listings. While she was sitting there fuming in a backed up traffic jam on the GWB, her phone went off. She didn't like to answer calls from numbers she didn't recognize, but since she wasn't going anywhere fast she answered it. "Hello who's calling?" The man's voice said, "Jazmyn?" At first she started to say "I asked who you were first." But she decided to give them a break. "Yes this is she. What can I do for you?" "Oh this is Mike, Monica said you wanted to talk to me." Jazmyn was relieved that he'd called, but now she started to feel a little uncomfortable.

Getting him to talk about his parents getting killed would be hard on him, but she didn't know what else she could do. There was no way to avoid it. To get the whole story, it had to come from him. After a pause she said, "Mike I really need to talk to you about what happened to your family before you and Monica came to New York. I know it's not something you want to think about, but I need to know what happened so I can figure out what I have to do. Is that going to be ok with you?" Mike got quiet for a second, then he said, "Hey Jazz, all I can promise is I'll do my best to tell you everything I can recall." She felt bad for him but she had to get things straight in her own head. "That's all I need from you Mike. I don't want to put you through anything that's too much, but this is important to me. Why don't we meet up in Port Authority? At least while we're talking in there everybody won't be all up in our business. When I get there I'll call you to let you know where to find me." "Ok I'll be there in about 30. Just let me know where to go. The way traffic is crawling it might be more like an hour." When Jazmyn looked in front of her she agreed with his estimate. "That's alright I'm stuck on the GWB, and I might as well be caught in a time warp. I could almost swear time or nothing else is moving on here." When Jazmyn finally got into Manhattan she parked on one of the side streets and hung her handicapped tag on the rearview mirror. She used it to throw off the parking police. She jumped out and quickly walked around the corner. She made her way along the crowded street, moving like she was a part of the giant swarm going into Port Authority. Before going inside she stopped to call Mike and let him know she was there. The call went straight to voicemail so she left this message. "Hi Mike, this is Jazmyn, I'm here waiting for you. Call me when you get here." She hung up and began taking a slow walk around the huge terminal.

There was something about being inside the Port Authority again that made her reminisce about the major decisions she'd made since coming to live in New York. They'd all seemed to culminate at the Port Authority some-how. She reflected on some of the choices she'd made and wondered if her plans of a future with Tango would ever be real. Here she was again, second guessing herself and the wondering whether her decisions were good. She still didn't know if they would lead to even more problems down the road. Deep down, she didn't know if what she was doing was the right thing for Mike and Monica. Mike was going to have to relive one of the most painful events in his life because she needed to know who was responsible for endangering their home. Was it even going to be worth it in the end? She was doing this to protect Tango and the future life they were meant to have. If this was what it was going to take, she couldn't stop halfway. Mike was going to have to go through this so Tango could catch Ellie's ass in her bull shit. Jazmyn hoped Mike would tell her something that would convince Tango to get rid of Ellie on sight. But she didn't know if getting rid of her would be good enough. Would it stop whatever trouble she could cause? She couldn't go to Tango with just what she'd heard on the phone. Ellie was too slick to fold with just that. Tango needed her so much she might be able to talk her way out of it. Jazmyn needed so much information Tango would have no other choice but to get rid of her. Then her phone went off and broke into her thoughts, it was Mike. "Hey Jazz where you at? I'm in here now." She looked up and saw the big M for McDonalds in front of her. "I'm up near the PATH tracks for Jersey at the McDonalds. I'll get a seat and wait for you in there ok?" "Alright, I'll be up there in a minute." Jazmyn got them both a cup of coffee and sat down in front to wait.

A few minutes later she saw him on the escalator and signaled him to come over. Mike sat down with a puzzled look on his face. "Okay Jazz, why don't you tell me what this is all about. Monica was acting like it was a secret mission or something." Jazmyn didn't know where to start, so she figured she just tell him what she didn't know. "Well Mike I'll tell you, I didn't know anything until I found a phone in Tango's office. I threw it in my purse and forgot all about it until it started ringing. I answered it, and somebody on the other end started cursing me out about something that happened in Florida 13 years ago. He said their brothers and father got killed and they were coming to New York to rob Tango. I got scared and thought you could tell me what happened." Mike didn't know how much he should tell or how much she wanted to know. But he was sure that he knew way more than she wanted to. "I'll tell you Jazmyn, when me and Monica first came here, it was like a Chinese fire drill. I was 16 and she wasn't nothing but a little thing, like 4 years old. See, Ellie used to come down and run a bunch of dope back up here to Tango. My moms and Marlon used to get it from the Columbians and get it ready for Ellie to bring back to Tango. The last time she came though things went way different. My mom and dad would go down to the beach to pick up the dope. That night I waited until they left, then I followed them down there. Before I left I made sure I took my 9mm with me. You know it's better to have it and not need it than need it and not have it. I wasn't supposed to go down there, but I was tired of always doing what they told me to do. Anyway, my dad never wanted me to get down with him on his moves. He didn't want me to hustle like him, but I wasn't a kid no more.

Jazmyn could tell by the way Mike was looking down at the table, that his story was getting to him. His fist was clenched tightly around the plastic stirrer the whole time as he went back through what happened. He kept going. "I laid down in the grass and watched them while they waited for the Columbians. After a little while I saw a small boat come with two guys in it. They threw Marlon a rope and he pulled them up on the beach. When they got out, the fat guy handed Marlon a book bag, and my mom gave the other guy the garbage bag she had with the cash in it. That's when some fools on a ATV rolled right up on them. The lights were out at first, but when they got closer they cut on some bright ass halogen lights. Everybody was blinded for a minute, but not me. I was in the grass behind them. When the two niggas in the back stood up, I could see they had some AR type rifles. They pointed them at everybody and said, "Drop everything and put your hands up." One of the dudes off the boat took off running up the beach. I guess he was trying to get away with the money, but they took two shots and hit him in the back. When they started shooting Marlon ran the other way to get out of the lights. That's when they both started shooting. I was shook at first, I didn't know what to do. I didn't want to make things any worse. But when they started shooting at Marlon, I started busting my gun. They couldn't tell where the other shots were coming from. Marlon got out of the lights, threw the bag of dope and rolled over busting off at them. The fat Columbian jumped behind the boat and tried to get out of sight, but one of them started shooting at him and my mother. When I saw that I moved from where I was and started busting at them again. I got the nigga that shot my moms and Marlon hit the driver. Then the last one jumped behind the ATV and started busting off at Marlon. I stopped shooting when Marlon got hit. That's when I knew I had to go hard.

I tried to get as close as I could so I could see where he was behind the ATV. I got a good shot and busted a cap in his ass. When I hit him I ran over there to make sure he was dead. Then I ran over to check on my mom. When I saw the hole in her chest I knew she was gone. I ran up the beach and got the bag of cash off the first Columbian. Then checked on Marlon. I knew he had got hit, but when I got closer I could see the top of his head was gone. I was so shook I couldn't do nothing but get the fuck out of there. I picked up his gun and put it in the bag with the dope. There wasn't nothing I could do but run back to the streets after that. I knew the police were on their way, and it wasn't gonna take them but a minute to get there. Aunt Ellie and Monica had to be going crazy after hearing all that gunfire. But I wasn't thinking about them, all I wanted to do was get back in the house. When I came in the back door, they was both looking shook. I hurried up and put Monica in the bed, then I showed Ellie the backpack and told her what happened. She was acting all weird at first, like she ain't even believe what I was telling her. Then she started acting like she thought somebody was gonna come after us. The next thing I know we had to get our stuff together, because she said we had to get out of there. I threw a bunch of me and Monica's clothes in a bag and we was out. We've been up here with Tango ever since.

"Jazmyn could hardly believe what she'd just heard. She knew for sure that Ellie was too dangerous to play around with. She had to move carefully too. "Mike I'm so sorry about everything that's happened to you and Monica. I wish I didn't have to make you bring it all up again." His fist was still clutching the stirrer, and Jazmyn knew it hadn't been easy for him to go back through that. She tried to reassure him. "But I don't want you to worry about anything ok? I'm going to take care of things from here. Just please don't say anything to Tango or your aunt about this. I've got to make sure this doesn't become an even bigger problem than it already is. Tango's got enough to take care of already, he doesn't need anything else to worry about. Promise me you'll let me take care of this. The only one you have to take care of is Monica" Mike just sat there, staring at the coffee as he slowly shook his head from side to side. It was like everything Jazmyn said was slowly sinking in. "Why don't you want me to tell Tango or anybody what we talked about? What am I supposed to do, walk around with all this shit on my mind and not say or do anything?" Jazmyn could see his heart had been broken, and she knew what he wanted more than anything was revenge for his parents. She could understand that, but she needed him to wait until it was the right time before he did anything like that.

She didn't tell him about the Jamaican accent, Ellie didn't need to find out about that. "We don't want to make it easier for Ellie to say anything to Tango that might make him believe she's still on his team. She is too dangerous to keep around and Tango is going to have to deal with her when he finds out everything about her." Even though he couldn't understand everything, Mike did know his aunt was a treacherous bitch. He didn't want to do it , but he promised Jazmyn, "I don't know what you think you can do about this, but I'll let you handle things your way, for now. But I'll tell you one thing, I feel like catching a case right about now." Even though he was smiling, Jazmyn sensed there was death and danger hidden behind his smile. That was probably something he'd been able to keep hidden. But after going over all this past trauma, it was like an itch he needed to scratch. Mike knew the other side of him was his worst self, but so far he'd been able to keep it in check. "Thank you Mike, I know this isn't easy for you. I wish I didn't have to ask you not to do what you feel is right, but you'll see that this is best in the long run. Mike wasn't thinking about any long run, all he could think about was what he had for the guilty ones. He didn't say how long he'd be able to keep his promise either.

When Jazmyn came back from meeting Mike she felt like a storm cloud was hanging over her head. She couldn't shake the feeling that she'd gotten herself in the middle of a big rotten mess. Not only that, now she had to protect the man she loved from danger when she couldn't know where it was coming from. How was she going to correct what she couldn't control? She'd put a lot of pressure on herself, and she couldn't rest until it was all straightened out. She hadn't told Mike the Jamaican had said Ellie's name. That wouldn't have helped anything. It probably would have just made matters worse. They'd already lost both their parents, how much worse would it be for Mike and Monica to find out their aunt was part of the reason it happened? That kind of news would have destroyed their whole world. She really felt bad for Monica, she'd already lost so much at an early age. It's really hard for a child to replace something they never had. It was a terrible thing for a little girl to lose their mother. Monica would never have what most people take for granted. But Jazmyn wasn't going to let herself sit around feeling sorry, she had to work on a way to get Ellie under control. How could she let Ellie know she wouldn't be under Tango's protection anymore? As she went over everything in her mind, she figured it was best to confront Ellie at her place. That way she could be sure Monica or Mike weren't going to be around. She spent a few more minutes trying to figure out why the password for her account still wasn't working. It kept failing until it finally locked her out of the company bank account. She decided not to wait any longer to get the Ellie business over with. She slammed the laptop closed and went down the hall to knock on Ellie's door. When she opened it Jazmyn said,

"Hey Ellie, come down to my place so we can talk in private for a minute. I need to know something and you're the only one who can tell me." Ellie looked confused, but curious. "Come on in Jazz, we can talk now. Nobody's here and I'm not expecting them back any time soon." But Jazmyn wanted this conversation to happen on her own turf. That way there wouldn't be any unwanted interruptions, and Ellie couldn't put her out if she wanted to. "No Ellie, let's talk down at my place. I want to make sure this is just between you and me." That really got Ellie's curiosity going. "Okay Jaz, I'll come down there as soon as I put the rest of this food up." Jazmyn turned on her heel and said, "That's cool, I'll be waiting on you." Then walked away without bothering to look back.

A few minutes later Jazmyn heard Ellie's almost timid knock on her door. As soon as Ellie came in she tried to take the lead in the conversation. "Alright now girl, tell me what you've got on your mind? When you first left I didn't know what to think." Jazmyn didn't feel like playing nice, in fact she wanted to pick up that big quartz ashtray and split Ellie's head with it. She could tell Tango they'd gotten into a fight and of course, he would believe and protect her. But she had to put that thought on hold for right now. Instead, Jazmyn drew a deep breath and started her interrogation. "Ellie, I wanted you meet me down here because I need to ask you about some things that happened before we met. Now, you can do whatever you want to do after this, but trust and believe, I'm not letting any of this shit go." Ellie's face was now showing her surprise and confusion. "I don't know what you're talking about Jazmyn, but I sure would like to find out. What have you got on your mind?" Jazmyn blinked her eyes real slow before she said. "Well, when you came here with Mike and Monica, weren't their parents killed in Florida?" She didn't need Ellie's confirmation, she just wanted her to think she still had some doubt about what actually happened. While Ellie was nodding her head she went on. "Well, I just found out the people who killed them know you. In fact, they've even been in contact with you." Ellie's face took on the expression of somebody who'd just been caught butt naked. But before she could say anything, Jazmyn went on. "These Jamaicans said they wanted to come here and rob Tango. They even said they might kill him as some kind of payback. All I want to know is what are you planning to do about any of that? You should know I'm not going to let anything happen to Tango. But what I can't understand is why you haven't already told him about this. Don't you think he would want to protect himself? You're crazy if you think I'm not going to let him know what you've been hiding from him. I want to know what you're going to do now that you know I know? Can you stand here now and answer my questions? Maybe try to convince me I'm wrong? Either way I don't have a problem telling Tango what I know. But one thing you can bet, is when he finds out you knew all along who these people were, he's not going to take it easy on you. Especially when he finds out that they want to rob him, he'll be looking at you in a whole new light. You should already know how he is, he's going to take things into his own hands. He's going to make sure he's protected, and that there's no weak links anywhere. You're the one in charge of his building, and you handle all his drug business. With your help they could take whatever they wanted."

While Jazmyn was busy laying out what she knew, Ellie's face had gone through all the phases from shock to anger to fear. Now her face was blank, and stuck on terrified. She tried her best to regain her composure, but it wasn't happening. "Girl I don't know where you're getting all this bullshit from, but I'll tell you one thing, you're dead wrong. How am I supposed to convince you you're wrong? Nobody wants to believe they're making a mistake. First they've got to see how wrong they are for themselves." Jazmyn's face showed nothing but contempt for the bullshit Ellie was trying to sell her. "Look Ellie, I wanted to keep things civil with you, but if you think I'm going to listen to you tell me lies and bullshit your way around this, you might as well stop talking now. All I can tell you is I hope the fantasy world you're living in can protect you, because when Tango finds out he's going to come back on your ass like a hurricane." Ellie knew her fake story and innocent act weren't getting her anywhere. She had to try something to buy some time. "Listen Jazz, I can see you're pissed off and want to protect Tango, but you're not thinking this through. No matter what you think happened in the past, Tango still trusts me. I've been taking care of his business for a long time, he knows I wouldn't do him wrong. Do you think you can just come out of nowhere and screw my life over with him? If you think he's going to go for that you're not as smart as you look. All I've got to do is tell him you're lying on me, he already knows you want to break up his whole operation so you and him can go off and play house. He knows you'd do anything to get him out of the game and you'd better believe I'll do whatever I have to do to protect myself. If you just use your head you could still end up with everything you want. But before that can happen you're going to have to let me get what I want too."

Jazmyn almost couldn't believe her ears. Was this crazy bitch trying to negotiate with her? Did she think she could still get what she wanted out of this? Jazmyn had to set her straight. "You must not know how close you are to Tango tearing your ass apart and using whatever's left for bait. The

Jamaicans called your phone and told me everything that happened. They also told me they're ready to do something to your ass about it." Ellie's brave front faded away when she heard the Jamaicans wanted to put hands on her. She looked panicked then "Listen Jazmyn, those Jamaicans are nothing but a pack of crazed dogs. They'll eat your kids and kill anybody that gets in their way. You don't know it but right now I'm the only thing standing between them and Tango. If I hadn't cut them off they would have already been here to do something." Jazmyn wasn't trying to get into a debate with her. "Listen Ellie, I talked to one of your Jamaican "friends" on this cell phone I found. He let me know you owed them and that they'll do something to you if you don't do what they want. You can't serve two masters. You're always looking for ways to come out on top of things." Ellie still wasn't ready to give up yet. She still tried to reason with Jazmyn. "I lost that phone over a week ago. If you found it in Tango's office you should know I thought I'd gotten away from them." Jazmyn rolled her eyes and with more than a little sarcasm said, "Yeah well, it's a good thing nobody's paying you to think. Now they know exactly where you are, and that makes you nothing but a liability around here. They want your help to work against Tango, and you already know I'm not going to let that happen. You can't be trusted around here anymore. If they show up here to do their dirt you'll do whatever they tell you to do."

Ellie didn't want things to end like that with Jazmyn. She had to stop her from being angry long enough to see how much was at stake. "Look Jazmyn, if those Jamaicans knew their way around New York they would have been here by now. If they had any idea where Tango's operation was they would have already tried to take him down. Don't you know if I was really working with them they could have done anything they wanted by now? After everything they've threatened me with, if I was really on their side Tango would already be fighting for his life. I've been lying and hiding from them so they couldn't find me. If they knew where I was they would have already robbed Tango's business. It's too late now to play dumb with them, when you answered the phone you let them know where I am. If I don't do something they'll come to New York. If they come here they'll do whatever they want and disappear back to Florida. Once they get back on their turf they'll be safe and protected by their crew. If things got too hot they could always go back to Jamaica." All Jazmyn kept thinking was, "This bitch is really sick in the head!"

Cocking her head to side Jazmyn told her, "You can't really be serious can you? You expect me to let you have even more time to do foul shit behind Tango's back? You act like I haven't been telling you what you've already been doing? Listen, I could let you settle this with Tango yourself." Jazmyn wasn't about to strike any bargains with her treacherous ass. This was going to have to be an all or nothing kind of deal with her. Since Jazmyn wasn't giving an inch, Ellie tried to put Tango in the mix. "Come on now Jazmyn think about it, Tango is a good man and I don't want anything to happen to him. I owe everything I've been able to do to him. The only way I got this far in the business was because of him. You've got to use your right mind to make the right decision. Why don't you and Tango take a vacation trip, go somewhere nice. Then while ya'll are gone the Jamaicans can rob his place. They'll only get what I leave there for them. Then they can get all that revenge shit out of their system and nobody will be in any more danger. By the time ya'll get back everything will be settled and I'll say I'm too shook up from everything to take care of business around here anymore. I swear, I'll leave here and won't ever come back. You don't have to worry about anything happening around here after that. You and Tango can be together and everything will be the way you want it." Jazmyn wasn't going to listen to anymore of the bull shit Ellie was trying to sell. She was already calculating her next move and what it was going to take to get rid of her ass. "Listen Ellie, it's too bad you got yourself caught up in some shit like this. Since you brought it all on yourself, I think it's time you took your medicine."

"You can start by growing up and accepting the fact that you're responsible for getting those kid's parents killed. Everything that happened out there that night was because of you. Your greed and treachery is what got you where you are today. They'll be harmed forever because you decided to be a greedy, lying, disloyal snake. Now do you think I'm going to make some kind of bargain with you? No thanks, it's not my job to help you come out of this shit smelling like a rose. You'd better talk to Mike and Monica about making a deal, because they're the only ones you should be asking to give your ass a break. Maybe they'll be willing to forgive you for what happened to their parents. Maybe you'll have a better chance with Tango, but I don't think you really want to go that route." Ellie still wasn't through, she had one more card to pull out of her bag of tricks. "Jazmyn, I told you these Jamaicans were ruthless, they'll do anything to get their revenge. The only thing on their minds is getting even. To them nothing is too much if they can get even for their family being killed that night. Ever since that happened they've been trying to get revenge. They'd like nothing better than catching up with Mike, and also getting Tango out of their way. Their wet dream is taking over his South Bronx terri-tory. If they could do that with their connections in Miami, they could stay supplied for life. If they got their hands on you and Devon, that would be all they'd need to get to Tango. Can't you see how you're putting everybody in danger because of your misplaced anger? Why are you creating all this drama over something that can't be changed? I really do wish things could have been different, but I didn't know what was going to happen out there that night. My sister got killed, I didn't want that. Why can't you at least let me talk to Tango myself. You owe me that much." Jazmyn didn't believe how fast she said it. Before she knew it the words were out, "Bitch, I don't owe your rotten ass a damn thing. You'd better hope Tango is as nice to your ass as you seem to think he'll be. If I was you I wouldn't bet my life on it."

"Since you have so much confidence in the time you've put in with Tango I'll give your ass three days to tell him everything about what the hell's been going on. If you haven't told him everything by Friday you'd better believe I'll be telling him all about it myself. Now get your ass out of my face, and I don't want you to say anything to me except goodbye." When Jazmyn opened the door Ellie knew she wouldn't be invited back. As Ellie walked away, the only thing on her mind was how she could keep her position safe. How could she get things back under control again? If she didn't stay on top of this, she might not make it out of there alive. It wasn't going to be easy, but nothing she'd ever done had been either. Three days could seem like a lifetime for some people. If she didn't come up with a plan, it could probably be the end of her life. Ellie sat on her bed wondering what to do and letting thoughts about what it would take chase any kind of sleep away. How could she escape the wreck she'd made out of her life? All she felt was despair about the situation, and the future she faced could only turn out bad. She had three days to figure out a way to keep Jazmyn from blowing her cover. If Jazmyn told Tango everything, she'd have no choice but to make a run for it. If she wanted to survive with her place in Tango's business, Jazmyn couldn't run to him with her story. If Jazmyn disappeared, that would solve everything for her. She only had three days to make her problems go away, but having a chance at all still gave her some hope. She was nervous and desperate, but she still had a chance to make something happen. She had to go to work and do her job, but at least there she'd have time to think. She needed to get rid of Jazmyn in a way that wouldn't point the finger back at her.

When the dope shipments came in Ellie's job was to keep track of the cut and mix process. That all went down in the basement where she was in charge of supervising every step in the process. The proper mixture was the last stage in getting it ready for the houses. The heroin this time was brown and moist, it was very potent. Once the workers had mixed in the cut and separated it into individual batches it was weighed and made into bricks. The cut they used didn't take much effect away from this dope. Even after they'd put a two on it, the dope was still very powerful and for that reason it had to be handled carefully. It was so strong they had to mix it more times than usual. They couldn't be too careful, too much pure dope in a batch could lead to a rash of OD's. That would make the block hot. If a junkie messed around and got too much in their system, there's no way they could survive it. Dead junkies didn't help sales at all. All that night the idea of what she needed to do was already in Ellie's head. All she needed was a way to put that idea into action. With a surgical mask over her face Ellie walked over to the pile of dope and scooped up about a teaspoon full and stuffed it down inside one of the glassine bags. Then she tucked that into her bra and walked away. No one there was going to question her or think twice about anything she did. Questioning the boss lady wasn't in their job description.

She walked around like that for the rest of the night. The only thing she could think about was how to get that pure dope into Jazmyn's system. She didn't have much time, and she wouldn't get too many opportunities to do what had to be done. They had to finish all the cutting and mixing in a day, so the dope could be compressed into bricks. When that was done, each of them would be weighed and wrapped up tight in several layers of clear plastic. They'd be wrapped and weighed again before they got delivered. Once the bricks were checked, reweighed and packed up, Mike and Alphonso took them to each of the houses. While they were gone Ellie's mind never stopped turning over and over with guilt, fear and uncertainty. Her fate would be twisting in the wind until she changed things and made it happen fast. The house was basically running on automatic pilot now. Anytime something came up she didn't even have to think about what to say, the answer was already in her head. When things came up that she didn't want to deal with, she put it off until the end of the night. It wasn't her conscience bothering her as much as what would happen to her if Tango found out about her deceit. She didn't even want to think about the kind of punishment and suffering he'd have in store for her. The sweat of desperation clung to her as she tried to convince herself she'd found a way out and everything was going to be alright.

Layla noticed how absent minded and disconnected Ellie was acting, so she said something about it. "Damn Ellie, are you feeling alright? I ain't never seen you dragging around here like this before. I've watched you work for 16 hours straight in a week and still kept my ass running. Is something wrong with you?" All she could do was force a weak smile and say, "Sometimes this shit just catches up with you, that's all. I'll be back right in no time. It only takes me a minute to regroup, that's all I need. Don't count me out yet, I've come back from worse things than this." Layla just nodded. "Alright, you know your program better than I do, I just hope you know when it's time to take a break that's all." She left it like that but she couldn't get the image of a tired Ellie out of her mind. "Why would she be so tired now? This is just Wednesday night. We're just getting started for the week, why would she be this tired already?" Layla couldn't shake the thought, and didn't buy Ellie s story either. They started their final count about 7:30 am. Ellie knew her plan had to get going so she needed Layla's help. "Can you stick around and do the last lock up for me? I'm tired, I need to get home and catch up on my sleep." "You know I've got you if you need me Ellie. I just hope you're alright, this ain't like you. When's the last time you were too tired to lock up? You'd better see a doctor and get checked out ok?" Ellie just shrugged and said, "I'll be alright once I catch up on my sleep." It would be Friday morning soon and Ellie knew that her tight schedule was only getting tighter. She still wasn't sure how she was going to take care of her problem. She just knew that it had to go down when she was nowhere around. The most important thing was it had to go down smooth. Ellie sat on her bed thinking, she only had a few options. Ellie couldn't stop thinking about what the rest of her life was going to be like, or if she'd even have any more life left if her plan didn't succeed.

Then she stood up and went over to look in the dresser drawer. That was where she threw all the junk she was always collecting. Rummaging through the clutter she came across an old set of keys. They were the ones she'd thrown in there when they'd first moved into the building. Her heart leaped when she recognized them, she thought these keys had been lost. They opened up every door in the whole building, except Tango's. He'd had his locks switched out when they redecorated his office and installed him a new door. Now, which one of those keys went to Jazmyn's door. A plan she'd only half believed in, was fast becoming a reality. She had the heroin, and now she had a way to get in her apartment. The hard part would be getting that dope in her system. How could she do it without anybody knowing it was her? This would be the hardest and most important part of the puzzle. If she didn't get this right, there weren't going to be any more second chances for her. Time was a relentless enemy, that never stopped closing in on her. She didn't have any to waste. It was a matter of life and death, and she had to get rid of Jazmyn before Friday. If Jazmyn got to Tango her life was going to be over. It was already Thursday afternoon, the pressure of time was closing around her neck like a noose. She squeezed her eyes closed, but still couldn't sleep. She was too wired and tense to even lay down. The battle in her mind was so intense she couldn't rest. Inside, all she felt was fear for her future. How could she not worry about her life? When Ellie got to work that night everybody could tell she wasn't herself. Instead of being busy and bossy, she was shaky and uncertain. Layla saw how she was acting and asked her about it again, "Hey Ellie, it don't look like you got enough sleep. Do you need me to take over things for you?" Ellie just said, "I could have used a little more, but the show must go on. That's why I'm in here, because the show don't stop." Layla took a good look at her and said, "You only get one chance to be you baby, and I bet you I ain't going to mess myself up for no job no how." Ellie didn't say anything to that, she just turned around and went back upstairs to her office.

After they exchanged those words Layla watched Ellie even closer. She couldn't help but notice how Ellie didn't look or act the same. Instead of giving orders and taking charge, she was acting unsure and insecure. She didn't exert authority like usual. When one of the girls asked her about something they were supposed to do she just told them and left it like that. Layla knew Ellie was a whole control freak. If somebody didn't know their job or did it right by now, she would have told them to go find a new one. But she wasn't taking charge of the people in there anymore. As the night went on, Layla noticed that Ellie was holed up in her office for most of it. The final money count didn't usually start until about 7:30 am, but around 4:30 Layla got a call from Ellie to come up and see her. When Layla got to the door she didn't bother knocking since she'd been called up there. When she walked in she saw Ellie with a razor in her hand, chopping a small pile of dope on the desk. When Layla saw her she froze. "My bad Ellie, I didn't know you were busy. I'll just wait out here until you're ready for me." Ellie looked up and said, "Don't be crazy girl, come on in here and close the door. I'm just checking the quality on this dope." After chopping on it a little more and sifting it to get any lumps out she said, "Layla I'm tired as hell tonight, I'm going to need you to close us down and lock up for me if you can. I've got to take care of some-thing very important. If you do this for me I'll give you next Saturday off with pay. That's a real busy day and I know you haven't had a weekend off since the last time I had one. So how about it, can you do that for me?" Layla was too shocked to say anything, she wasn't used to getting so much good news at one time like that. "Hell yeah I'll close down for you.

Who's gonna turn down the chance to run the club and have a Saturday off with pay?" She was still smiling when she said, "Girl, I told you a long time ago if you ever needed me I'd be there. I remember when you put me in charge of the girls upstairs, you knew I could handle that shit before I did." Layla noticed Ellie smiling as she talked, but never once did she stop chopping up the dope. When she did stop all she said was, "Thanks Layla, I'll always have your back after this. If there's ever anything I can do to help you out around here just ask." When Layla got back upstairs to the girls she couldn't understand what had happened to change her fortunes so fast. She sure wasn't looking a gift horse in the mouth, it was about time she had some good luck. Ellie left the building soon after that and didn't say a word to anybody. She would usually check on things and make sure things were good before she left, but not this time. Tonight she just grabbed her stuff and took off fast.

The only thing on Ellie's mind was making sure her plan worked. There was no two ways about it, if she didn't do what she had to do, she was going to have to find a new way to keep breathing. When Ellie got home Monica was in bed asleep, Mike wasn't even there yet, so she went straight to her room and got the ring of keys she needed. Quickly she crept down the hall and stopped at Jazmyn's door. She nervously tried each of the keys until one finally turned in the lock. Even though her heart was pounding, she couldn't stop. She slowly pushed the door open and slipped inside. Standing there in the hallway she hurriedly slipped off her shoes and tip toed down the hallway to Jazmyn's bedroom. By now she was breathing hard in a panic. She leaned against the wall to take the time to calm her nerves. She took out the bag of dope and opened it. She took out a flexible straw she'd taken from behind the bar earlier. She stuck that down in the heroin and stuffed as much as she could in the end. She had chopped up so fine it easily went into the straw. Then Ellie took a breath and went in Jazmyn's room. At this moment, she was more frightened than she'd ever been in her life. She moved forward quietly until she stood over Jazmyn's sleeping body. She took in a breath and put the end of the straw loaded with heroin into Jazmyn's nose. With a short quick blast of air, she sent all the dope up into her nose. When Jazmyn didn't react right away, Ellie hurriedly filled the straw and did the same thing to her other nostril. Then Jazmyn turned her head and started coughing. The sudden movement scared Ellie so much she dropped the straw and quickly crouched down next to the bed. Ellie was so panicked she almost dropped the bag of dope too. Jazmyn sneezed and started to shake, but she still hadn't woke up. Then Ellie heard sounds coming from Devon's room next door. She was already scared, but that made her lay down on the floor. She was so scared of being caught she stayed as still as a stone. When she heard him walking in the hall it sent her into an all out panic. She wished she could have melted into the floor, but all she could do was slide under the bed and pray that he didn't walk in. She kept moving under the bed until she was sure she was out of sight. The sound of footsteps in the hall had her heart pounding in her chest. She stopped breathing when he walked past the door. She let her breath out after he passed by. He was only going to the bathroom. She closed the bag of heroin and slipped it in the pocket of Jazmyn's nightgown laying on foot of the bed. Devon walking by scared Ellie so much, she knew it was time to get out. When she heard him in the bathroom, she took a chance and made a break for the door. She had to get out while he was in the bathroom. She couldn't let herself relax until she was back in her apartment. In there, she closed her bedroom door and all the tension she'd been feeling drained out of her. It still wasn't over, but there wasn't anything else she could do. As daylight started to creep through her window she knew it was going to shed light on the dirt she'd done in the dark. It seemed like hours had gone by, but the chaos of her mind didn't keep up with the time. She never fell asleep. All she did was worry and wonder if she would have a chance to live the rest of the week. She really didn't see a future for herself anymore, all she could do was keep breathing in and out. She envisioned some things that could happen, but those were nightmares that only took her mind deeper into panic and despair.

Then came the day Devon was never going to forget. It had started out like any other day, at least that's what it seemed like. Like every other day he got up and got out like he was "going to school." Leaving the house fast was a good way to avoid a bunch of questions from his Mom about school. He spent most of the day at the pool room and the rest of it with Keith roaming Manhattan's busy streets. By the time he got home it was a little after 4:00 pm. He came in the front door thinking his mom was somewhere around. He yelled out, "Mama! I'm home." when she didn't answer, he went in his bedroom and changed into some different clothes. It was another habit he'd gotten into. Whenever he came in he'd change his clothes so he wouldn't be wearing his "school" clothes around all day. When he was done changing he wondered why he didn't smell anything cooking. That was real unusual so he called for her again. This time when she didn't answer he came out of his bedroom to see where she was. When he got to the living room he froze in his tracks. He saw was his mother lying there sprawled out on the living room floor. But when he saw how her eyes looked, it really froze his heart. They were wide open, staring but not seeing him. Her eyes were frightening because they were frozen in place and motionless. Their empty glaze told him she couldn't see anything. In a few seconds he went from confusion and shock to fear and panic. He shook his head to get himself out of it and ran over where she was. When he picked up her head the sensation of cold really struck his mind. The sensation of coldness snatched away any hope he had that she might still be alive. He couldn't believe how cold she felt. Her skin like she'd been carved out of a piece of ice. Even though he knew she was dead, his heart wouldn't let him accept what that meant. More than anything, what he felt the most was lost and confused. He didn't know what he was supposed to do. How was he supposed to deal with the sadness taking over his mind? It was too late to help her, but something had to be done. The tears in his eyes blurred his vision before he knew what they were. In that time, the world stopped mattering to him. None of his thoughts were coherent as he sat there holding her head in his lap.

When he snapped out of it he didn't know how long he'd been sitting there. Devon laid her head back on the floor, and like a zombie went down the hall to Ellie's door. Standing there knocking, the reality of his mother's death started to dawn on him. When Monica opened the door, she took one look at him and could see that something was wrong. "Dee, what's the matter with you? Why are you looking like that? Come in here and sit down. Tell me what's going on." He came in, but Devon never said a word. He just sat on the couch and stared off into space. Ellie came out of her bedroom to see who had come in. "What's wrong with him? Is he sick or something?" Monica just shrugged her shoulders. "I don't know what's wrong with him, but something definitely ain't right. He just came in here with this blank look on his face. He ain't said nothing since he came in here." Ellie grabbed Devon by the shoulders and gently shook him back and forth. When she saw that he was focused on her she asked him, "What's wrong with you boy! Tell me what's the matter with you." All he kept saying is, "My mama's dead. My mama's dead." Ellie said "What? Where is she Devon? Where?" Devon didn't answer, he just cast his eyes in the direction of the door. Ellie ran down the hall to Jazmyn's apartment as fast as she could. When she saw that the door was still open, she went inside. Jazmyn's body was still on the living room floor where Devon left her. Her relief was mixed with only a slight amount of guilt. She didn't like seeing herself as a killer, but she wasn't going to worry about that. Without hesitating Ellie picked up the telephone and dialed 911.

Before she left Jazmyn's apartment she looked around to make sure she didn't see anything that could incriminate her. She went in Jazmyn's bedroom to see if there was anything in there. She got the bag of dope out of Jazmyn's nightgown and wiped it clean before putting it back. She didn't need her fingerprints on that. Then she checked for any kind of clues that might lead back to her. After she was sure nothing in there that could tie her to the death, she closed the door and went back down the hall. On her way, she started planning how she was going to handle things. There would be a lot to get done, and Monica would have to take responsibility for Devon. Whatever happened at Jazmyn's was probably going to be up to her. Ellie usually took care of whatever happened around the building. She was the one Tango held responsible for what happened there. This wouldn't be any different. She was going to be kept busy answering questions about what happened. Not just from the police but from nosey neighbors too. Naturally there'd be a lot of speculation about what happened and who knew what. All she wanted was to make sure her name was mentioned as little as possible. When Ellie's thoughts were organized in her head, she started barking out orders. "Monica, get you a cold wash cloth and wipe that boy's face off. He's gonna have to snap out of it and get himself back together. When the police get here they're going to want to talk to him, and he's gonna need this mind sharp to answer their questions. You've got to keep an eye on him and see if he knows what happened to his mama. Do you hear me?" Ellie was in full control mode now. That's something she was used to since she'd been running things for Tango so long. It was only natural for her be the one that kept everything together.

She called Tango to let him know what happened to Jazmyn and there was a strange silence on the phone. After a few seconds he said, "I'm on my way there, and don't let anybody touch anything." But before Tango could get there, the police had already come. They started a so called investigation, but they didn't seem too interested in what happened to Jazmyn. They seemed more interested in everything else happening at the building. The homicide detectives didn't give anything their full attention. It only took them about 30 minutes to find out everything they wanted to know about. They looked for signs of forced entry and asked everybody if they heard anything unusual or saw anything out of the ordinary. They basically continued their long running practice of being a pain in everybody's ass. When they finally stopped asking pointless and unproductive questions the coroner came. They took a bunch of pictures, examined her body and put her in a body bag. While they were busy taking care of whatever other business they had, they made small talk with the detectives. Standing around being nosey was what most of them had to do. The main thing they wanted to do was stay out of sight. It took them a few hours to move her body out and essentially close the book on the case. Except for a few shocked looks and a lot of head shaking, things went pretty much back to normal. Tango had come over to make sure nobody got in the way of the police. Plus he didn't want them trying to use her death as an excuse investigate any further than they had to. He was surprised at how quickly they handled everything. Nobody would have believed that. Tango purposely stayed up on the third floor while the police did their jobs. He didn't want to get in their way, but if they had needed to talk to him for anything he was right upstairs. Tango figured if he let them do their jobs, they wouldn't have to come back. He didn't show any emotion, but everybody knew he wasn't going to take her death too well.

Whenever anything went down around there that wasn't planned ahead of time, Tango was the man in charge. If he wasn't personally calling the shots he made sure somebody that answered to him was, and that was usually Ellie. Overseeing what happened in the building was how he main-tained control over his people and his property. That day you could tell Tango was only there physically. You could see him, but he wasn't being his normal self. Anybody who knew how he really was, would have known there wasn't any real life in him. His mind was wrestling over one question, one he'd asked himself over and over again. Ever since he heard Jazmyn was dead, all he wanted to know was how? They would have to wait for the autopsy before they'd know the cause of death. There weren't any signs of foul play, and the police and their entourage had came and left in a matter of hours. Ellie tried to answer as many of the neighbors questions as she could. She even filled out the police report with as many facts about Jazmyn as she knew. Whenever there was confusion or uncertainty, it was her habit to try and appear to be the most competent and informed person around. She prided herself on being who you had to deal with whenever any kind of information or knowledge was needed. She handled Jazmyn's death with just the right amount of sympathetic care and efficiency. From the police to the neighbors, Ellie did her job and kept things moving along. It had taken a few hours, but Devon was starting to come back to himself. Monica made sure he didn't leave until Ellie said it was alright. He wanted to lay down on the couch but Monica wouldn't let him. She kept bugging him to get in the bed, until she finally talked him into laying down in Mike's room. Monica stayed in there with him, rubbing his head with a cold cloth and telling him things were going to be alright. Eventually, he went to sleep. When Ellie got back from Jazmyn's the first thing she did was get Monica. "You need to leave Devon alone. Stop messing with him and go down to Jazmyn's place. I need you to clean things up in there as fast as you can. Get a bucket with some rags so it can get cleaned up like it's supposed to be. Monica wasn't feeling that shit and didn't have no trouble letting her know it. "How come I'm always the one doing all the cleaning? I don't see why somebody else can't do it. Pay one of them girls that work at the club, or you could do it yourself." Ellie wasn't about to put up with no extra noise from her hot ass. "Listen to me little girl, you're going to do what I said because I'm telling you to do it. That's all the reason you need if you want to know why. How many more reasons do you need? Now get that stuff like I told you to and be ready by the time I come back."

The look Monica gave her would have killed her if it was a

gun. Before she got ready to leave, Monica bent down to Devon's ear and whispered, "Baby, when I get old enough, me and you are going to be out of here. Just don't you never forget that I'm the one you need." Then she put a big wet kiss on his forehead and left. As she started to getting the stuff to clean with, she couldn't help wondering why Ellie was so worried about getting Jazmyn's place cleaned up. When she was ready with all the cleaning stuff Ellie came down to Jazmyn's too. "Make sure you clean up everything in here, from her bedroom to the kitchen. I want that bedroom cleaned up first, and I mean clean in there until it shines, I don't want to see no fingerprints or anything else out of place in there." That's something that made Monica wonder, why was she so worried about getting Jazmyn's bedroom cleaned up ? Wasn't nobody gonna be going in her bedroom. All of that kept her thinking, "That Ellie is sure one strange bitch." As she was busy cleaning up in there, Monica couldn't help thinking about everything Ellie had said. Why did the bedroom need to be cleaned up so much? Why was the bedroom the first place she wanted cleaned? Monica knew there had to be a reason why, so she started looking for that reason. Something had to explain why Ellie was acting so weird. She didn't know what she was looking for, but Monica had a feeling it was there. The more she wiped and straightened things out, the more atten-tion she paid to them. While changing the linen, she saw a drinking straw on the floor behind the headboard. She picked it up and noticed one end was all crusty. There wasn't anything to drink out of around so she stuck it in her pocket. She didn't know why a straw would be in there if there wasn't anything to drink. When she was finished wiping everything down, she took a break. That's when she went in Jazmyn's closet, fantasizing about owning some of the fine furs and fabrics in there. She imagined the clothes were hers, as the colors and textures mesmerized her. She got lost in the fragrance and texture of all of the furs and fine silks. Her skin was tantalized by their smooth and seductive softness. Monica loved the way everything felt on her skin, until something coarse and stiff scraped across her face. That shook her out of her fantasy. It was something in one of the jacket pockets. She found what it was, and pulled out a small envelope that was addressed to Tango. She could see there was a note inside.

She couldn't resist the urge so she opened it up:

> Tango,
> I know things between us haven't always been good, but you've never had to doubt my loyalty or my love. I'm writing this because it means everything to me that you protect yourself. I understand sometimes you have to do the things you do to stay safe. What I tell you is going to make you angry but just know that I'm telling you because it's for your own good. Ellie is a snake. She's planning on helping some Jamaicans rob your numbers and drug stash. They even said they wanted to kill you if you tried to stop them. I found a phone in your office couch and some Jamaican guy called it. He thought I was Ellie so he was talking about a robbery in Florida that went bad 13 years ago. He said Ellie owed them everything she had, and it was time for her to pay them back. He said they were coming to New York to rob your numbers bank and drug stash. I'm afraid for you. I know you'll do whatever you have to do about this. I'm telling you about it because I didn't want to know about this and

not say anything.

I just hope you don't do anything that will make things worse for us and our future together. You know this kind of life isn't right for me and you. You know I've been waiting so long for you because I knew you'd see one day that our time would have to be sooner instead of later. Don't let this throw our dreams out the window again. Now that things are better between us it makes the future bright for us again.

I'm going to wait until I know more before I tell you anything else.

With all my love,

Jazmyn

Monica couldn't believe what she read. She was standing there in shock trying to figure out what to do next when she heard the front door open. "Monica!" It was Ellie. Monica quickly tucked the note in her back pocket and said, "I'm in here cleaning up. What is it?" Monica heard her walking down the hallway and quickly picked up a cloth and started wiping off the table. "I'm almost done cleaning in here." Ellie came in the bedroom looking all around at everything and said, "You still ain't done in here? I thought you would have the whole damn house done by now." Monica's voice took on a surly tone. "If you was in that much of a hurry you should have done it yourself." Ellie shot her a disapproving look and said, "Don't you worry about me, just make sure you're in here doing what you're supposed to be doing." Monica sneered back, "Yeah, ain't I always?" Ellie looked like she wanted to leave but didn't want to be gone. Monica said, "Can I get out of here now? It's clean enough in here, I need to get down to the bar so I can make me some money. I've got some of the girls down there waiting to pay me for doing their hair tonight." Ellie looked at her like she was speaking Greek. "You don't have to worry about that, you need to stay here and keep your eyes on Devon. I don't want you leaving him by himself for a few days, at least not until he looks like he's got himself back together. Monica felt like saying something else, but since it was just gonna start another argument she smacked her lips and rolled her eyes. Before Ellie could say anything else to piss her off she was down the hall and out the door. The note and the straw had filled her mind with a lot of burning questions. She was going to have to talk to her brother, he'd tell her exactly what to do. As soon as he got home she was going to tell him about everything she'd found. As soon as she got back she went and checked on Devon. When she saw him laying there sleeping peacefully, her heart dripped out to him. Looking at him quiet and calm, she couldn't help thinking, "This is probably the only time he'll ever look innocent." Her heart was smiling inside as she quietly closed the door.

Monica knew she couldn't tell Devon about what she'd found. The only one she could trust with that was her brother. Ever since they'd gotten to New York, he'd protected her. Going from Florida to New York on a Greyhound bus was no small thing for a five year old. The whole trip she'd been afraid of everything. He kept trying to tell her about all the things they passed along the way, but she hadn't cared about any of it. All she wanted to do was stay under him. That's the only way she wouldn't be scared again. Mike had kept her safe, and he made her feel secure too. Just by being there, he made her believe they were going to be alright. Even aunt Ellie knew better than to take things too far with him. He was known for going off when people pressed him or pissed him off. She'd only seen him go off once, but after that people didn't want it happen again. She called his phone, and he had to answer it like a smart ass. "What you want Chicken little? This had better be good because I'm in the middle of some-thing. What's up?" Monica turned on her baby voice. "Mikey I really have to talk to you. You're the only one I can talk to about this. It's something big, when are you coming home?" "I'll probably be there around ten or something like that. Just keep yourself together until I get there alright?" Monica said, "I'm alright now big bro. Stay safe out there." "I'm good, the rest of the world better look out for me. Peace" Click.

When Devon started moving around it wasn't easy for her to keep the secret she had. She hid everything in her dresser and tried to act normal. It's crazy, but she felt like she was being a creep. She didn't like keeping stuff about his mother from him, but she had to see what Mike said about it first. She went over to where he was sitting up and said, "I'm sure glad you woke up, you could help me get my stuff down to the bar. Don't you want to help me make some money tonight?" Devon didn't answer her at first, he just kept on looking out the window. He was still thinking of things and how much he'd lost. Out of nowhere he asked, "Where'd they take my mama's body to? I want to see her before they start doing all that funeral home shit to her. I don't want to see how she's gonna look after they done made her face up and all that." Monica was shocked when he asked her about that. Since she was the only one there, it was on her to tell him something. "I don't really know what's happening with all that, you're going to have to ask aunt Ellie when she gets back. She's been taking care of everything." Devon nodded his head and kept staring out the window. Monica pulled his arm to get his attention.

"Come on now Dee, I need you to help me out. You're always saying I could depend on you right? I could get some good money if you help me out. If you don't help me get my supplies down there I'm gonna miss out. I can't get my stuff down there by myself." When he looked at her she thought he had a strange look on his face. "You know I'd never let you down if you really needed me. Tell me what you need, then watch and see if I don't do it." She didn't really need his help, but she had to keep him occupied. The way she saw it she was killing two birds with one stone. He looked her again and this time he smirked her. She could tell he wasn't feeling doing any of that shit. Reluctantly Devon nodded his head, but when he did he said, "Yeah alright, but this kind of shit is not in my job description. You should know after this you're going to owe me your life.

Devon and Monica didn't make it back from the bar until after midnight. When she saw Mike's bedroom door closed she knew Mike had already been there. He was gone again and she still hadn't talked to him. Devon stood there looking lost with her bags and hair supplies. He put them down by the door and said, "Yo kid, I'm getting out of here. I've got to go home one day. Waiting around isn't going to make it any easier. I might as well just get it over with now. I'm going to go back home tonight." Monica didn't want him to leave her there by herself. She was supposed to be keeping an eye on him. "Damn Dee, you could at least stay until my brother come home. I don't want to be up in here all by myself." He didn't look like he cared about that. Devon still looked tired, even though he'd slept most of the day away. "You'll be alright, as much as you run your mouth you'll probably talk yourself to sleep. I'm going home and go to bed." With that he walked out and left her there by herself. She couldn't do anything but go in her room and lay there on her bed. She let imaginary scenarios and outlandish possibilities keep her wide awake. She was going to be awake when Mike came home, she wasn't sleepy anyway. She didn't know if she couldn't sleep because of what was in her dresser, or because she was worried about Devon. She didn't know if he'd really be alright by himself down there. Whatever it was, she couldn't go to sleep. It was around 5:30 when she heard her aunt Ellie come in. The thought of what she could have been up to sent a chill through her. She might have even been a little scared.

It was almost 7 o'clock in the morning when Mike finally came in. When she heard him in his room, she crept out her door and tip toed down the hall. She knocked quietly on his door. As soon as he opened it, Monica rushed inside and pressed her finger against his lips. Whispering she said, "Big bro listen to me, I found something down at Jazmyn's that's straight crazy. I didn't know what I was supposed to do with it, that's why I waited on you. I know you'll figure out what needs to happen. You've just got to tell me what I need to do." Mike knew his sister, she could get psyched up real quick over nothing. He grabbed her by the shoulders and shook her to make her stop talking. When she stopped he looked in her eyes and said, "Listen little girl, there's nothing we can't deal with together alright? Now calm your ass down and tell me what's going on." Monica was still whispering when she said, "I found something crazy while I was cleaning up Jaz's house. Don't none of this look right to me." She pulled out the sand-wich bag with the straw and note inside and handed it to him. Once he had it she felt like a giant weight was lifted off her. It was in his hands, and now the pressure wasn't hers anymore. He read the note then tasted the stuff caked on the end of the straw. Then he slowly started shaking his head back and forth.

All he said was, "That bitch did do it. After all this time, every-thing makes sense." Monica was clueless, but seeing her brothers reaction made her skin crawl. She already knew he had a crazy temper, but when she saw his veins bulging out like that she knew he was ready to go off. "What's the matter bro? What's happening? Tell me what I'm supposed to do. How come don't nobody never to tell me nothing?" Mike thought about how all of this could affect his sister, and that calmed him down. He looked at her, deciding how much she needed to know. All while he was thinking over exactly what he should say. "Listen Moni, I know you don't remember when we first came here. Everything was happening fast and you was still real little. That's how we ended up on the bus and coming up here to live with Tango and Ellie. Everything in this note is proof. Ellie was down with what happened to Marlon and mama. Now you have to listen to me, don't get it twisted. I'm going to take care of all of this. But from now, I want you to stay as far away from Ellie's ass as you can get.

Down the hall Devon turned the key in the apartment door for the first time without his mom there. It was just his apartment. For a split second he wished he could forget everything about the last day. What happened would always be his worst memory. But he knew that wasn't going to ever happen. He was going to have to put that away in the back of his heart like an open wound. It almost felt like he was home again, but the feeling only lasted a second. Instantly the feel-ings of emptiness and sadness he'd been fighting off came over him again. They squeezed him and settled around his heart like a cloud full of misery. When his legs started to buckle he quickly sat down at the dining room table. He stayed there until he felt his strength come back. He wondered if he could keep living there without his mother.

Sitting there looking around, he started feeling like he was weak and sorry for himself. He gave himself those few minutes for everything to wash over him. Then he remembered that his life hadn't always been full of trouble. He wasn't going to sit there and cry over memories of his mother. She hadn't given him anything to be sorry about. Everything she'd taught him would always be his. He was always going to know how sweet she'd been and how much she'd cared and tried to correct him. Those things were his forever. She wasn't there in person to give them anymore, but they were still deep down inside of him. He hadn't listened to a lot of what she told him because he didn't want people to think he was soft.

Now he'd have to make it in the world without her. Who was going to be the strong backbone for him? Now he was going to have to be the man she was trying to make of him. Could he stand up and be his own man now? Was he ready to take the ups and downs without crying for somebody to come and save him? No matter what, he'd have to handle everything on his own. He stood up and walked around the apartment, looking at all the things his mom had done to turn it into a home.. His mother's style was everywhere, from the curtains to the table cloth. Everywhere he looked he saw her personality. They reminded him of her, but they were also all that remained of her. But that didn't make him sad, it made him feel like in a way she was still there with him. Suddenly he felt at peace, like his mother really was still there. When he finally laid down to sleep, a million thoughts tried to fill his mind all at once. But what was really funny is, the last thing he saw before he went to sleep was Monica's face.

Since Jazmyn died, Ellie had been running back and forth like she was on some kind of speed. Tango was both impressed and relieved at how Ellie took over Jazmyn's burial arrangements. Tango told the funeral home he was taking care of all the expenses, so she didn't have any trouble setting things up. Everybody was wondering why Ellie was so concerned, that puzzled everybody. The whole neighborhood knew her and Jazmyn were far from the best of friends. Tango wasn't the type to get too close to anyone unless there was something in it for him. The way him and Jazmyn were you would have thought they'd grown up together. Her and Tango had a history, but not the hearts and flowers kind. Ever since Jazmyn moved into the building people had seen how jealous and petty Ellie could be. Everybody knew it was really about Tango. Jazmyn and Ellie both wanted to establish where they stood with him. Even though Ellie had been with Tango the longest, she'd never been more to him than a valuable employee. She wanted more than that, but he never gave that a thought. All Tango cared about was taking care of his business. Ellie did everything she could for Tango, but no matter how much she did, or how many times she bent over backwards, he never gave her the kind of attention she wanted. Maybe taking care of Jazmyn's burial was her way of trying to keep herself in his good graces. Whatever it was, nothing could make Tango feel good after he saw that autopsy report. About a week later the report said Jazmyn's death was the result of a heroin overdose. She'd ingested enough pure heroin to shut down her nervous system. The shock it had to her circulatory and respiratory system caused them to breakdown. That break down resulted in her death. This was a complete shock to everyone who knew her. Everybody knew Jazmyn didn't use drugs, and she definitely didn't use heroin.

Tango took this news the hardest. He had the hardest time accepting it too. Jazmyn didn't have any kind of drug history, so it wasn't possible for anyone that knew her to believe she'd overdosed on heroin. That autopsy report created a lot of speculation and uncertainty. The fact that she never used drugs was kept from the police. Telling the police that would have just attracted more of their attention on the building and what went on there. Tango couldn't give the police more reasons to be worried about what went on there. They would have just used that as an excuse to focus more of their attention on everybody there. Nobody needed that to happen. The funeral and everything else passed without Tango making a fuss about anything. Everybody still knew he was boiling inside. How could somebody that didn't use any drugs get enough heroin to die from it? Questions about how she died and what happened for Jazmyn to die like that ate away at Tango. He was thinking about what happened to her so much he could hardly stand being around the building. He didn't have anybody to talk to or confide in. He was the only one who knew what was going on in his head. Everything around there seemed to somehow remind him of Jazmyn. In the end, he knew he had to get away. The strain of trying to focus on running his operation, while wondering about what happened to Jazmyn, that went down right under his nose, was taking a toll on him. The daily grind of business and knowing that somebody in his circle was that treacherous and sinister, wore him down. One day he decided he didn't want to take it there anymore. He packed a suitcase and had Mike drive him to the airport. He didn't tell anybody where he was going, or when he'd be back. That he left the way he did meant he wasn't giving anybody a chance to stop him or question him about what he was doing. As far as anybody knew he'd just dropped out of sight.

Tango went down to the Florida Keys and settled in at the

Key West Casa Marina hotel. Nothing was more most important than getting back to his right mind. He didn't even know
if he wanted to keep living the kind of life he'd made for
himself. For the first three days all he did was lay on the beach
getting drunk in the sun. He drank so much rum on the
beach, the hotel didn't want to keep serving him. He tipped
the little waiter who brought it to him until he could barely
walk. On the last day of his all day drinking session, a pretty
young girl came jogging his way. He'd been stuck out on the
beach and was so far gone from the rum he didn't think he
could make it back to his room by himself. He didn't have
anything to lose so he gave it a try. "Excuse me miss, could
you help me out for a minute? I just want to ask you a question." The girl stopped, but kept jogging in place as she came
over. "What is it? I'm in the middle of my run but I'll help if I
can." Tango said, "I'm sorry for stopping your run, but could
you get somebody from the hotel to come down here to help
me get back to my room? I think I might have had a few too
many drinks." While she was there, she took the time to get a
better look at the man. She could tell by his manicured finger-
tips and Gucci link chain he was just the kind of somebody
she should get to know a little bit better. "Alright, don't worry
about a thing. I'll get somebody to come down here and get
you in a minute alright?" Tango nodded his head in agreement
before starting to nod off again. When she saw the way his
head was bobbing up and down she said, "Now don't go to
sleep on me alright? You've got to stay awake or nobody can
get you back to your room." She put her hands behind his
head and propped it up saying, "Now come on and sit up.
You've got to let me know you're alright before I leave Ok?"

When Tango felt the heat from her soft fingers on his neck
he opened his eyes up. "Oh don't worry about me little girl,

I've been in worse spots than this before, and as you can see I'm still kicking." She doubted it but humored him anyway. "Well I'm going to have to trust you on that, but when the men from the hotel get here you're going to have to tell them Kim wants them to call her room because she wants to make sure you got in alright, Okay?" Tango tried to sit up a little more when he heard her name. Tango said, "Kim said call her room? If they call you how are you going to know who they're talking about?" When she saw the way he was smiling she started to wonder how drunk this nigga really was. "I'm just trying to make sure you get back to your room alright. Ok Mr. smart ass, what is your name? In case I need to file a dirty old man report on you." Now she was the one smiling. All she was thinking was, "Either he's drunk as a skunk or he's kicking pimp game at me." Tango tried to shake off the effects of how drunk he was and said, "My name is Tango Mitchell honey, and I'll be alright once I get off this damn beach. Now Kim, can you please go and get me that help? I really don't know how much longer I'll be able to stay awake out here." She doubted how true that was but said, "Alright I'm going now, are you sure you can remember my name? What is it again? Tango said, "It's Kim and I'm going to make sure they call you after I get back to my room."

When he woke up the next morning Tango had a world's record level hangover. The pain in his head was like nothing he'd ever felt before. After a long slow shower he got dressed and made his way down to the patio by the pool. Once he got settled, he ordered a tall glass of orange juice along with a pot of black coffee. Sitting there in the sun and in a daze, he tried his best to organize his thoughts. The main thing on his mind was getting to the bottom of Jazmyn's murder. Thinking and scheming with a colossal sized headache was not what the doctor ordered. He was about to go back up to his suite and lay down when he felt the gentle touch of a hand on his shoulder. He turned around and saw his Bay Watch rescuer. She was standing there in a bright white sun dress that was barely hugging the curves of her womanly frame. Once his eyes had adjusted to the sunlight again he was treated to a very warm and beautiful smile. "Well good morning there Mr. Mitchell. I'm happy to see that you're up and out of your room. I'm even happier you're not drinking anything alcoholic today. The way you looked yesterday I wouldn't have bet money I'd see you again." Tango made a feeble attempt to smile before he said, "You should know better than to judge a book by its cover, I'm tougher than I look. It'll take more than a few too many drinks to finish me off. If you were any kind of a guardian angel you'd be saving me from this hangover. Why don't you join me? Then I could get to know my rescue angel a little better. I would like to know what made you decide to save me of all the emergency cases you have to attend to." She did want to know what he had in mind, but there were still a few things she had to take care of before she could do what she wanted. "I'd love to sit here and relax with you, but I've got take care of the little bit of business this morning. If you're still around we can get together later and talk. Maybe then I can find out a few more things about you before I decide if I should trust you or not." Tango liked the sound of what she was talking about and said, "Sounds like we've got a date if that's not too much to hope for." Tango gave her a wink and tried his best to smile, even though it hurt a little. His mind was already on some recreation as he watched her walk away.

He surprised himself for even thinking about catching up with that hot piece of ass, but he didn't see how getting into a situation with her could get him into any kind of trouble.

With that he sat back and took another swallow of black coffee. He was going to need his mind to be straight later on. The only thing he'd been thinking about before she came over had been the hot mess he'd left in the Bronx. He had to find out how the heroin had gotten into Jazmyn's system. That was the question that had been eating him alive. Somebody had to have given it to her, but who, and why? That was the point he was at, and it may as well have been the middle of nowhere. Tango wasn't going to figure out who and why unless he figured out who would have had a motive to do something like that. The whole thing didn't make any sense to him, and he wasn't letting the question stay unanswered much longer. When he was headed back up to his suite instead of another day of being drunk on the beach, he decided to go to the front desk. "Excuse me, there's a young lady registered here named Kim, she helped me get back to my room yesterday do you know who I mean?" The clerk had a sly smile on his face when he answered. "I sure do Mr. Mitchell, she called down this morning to ask if you were alright." Tango thought, "I must have been on her mind more than she let on." He told the clerk, "Put the rest of her expenses on my card for the time she stays here alright?" He handed the clerk his black card and said, "You don't need to tell her, I'll break the news to her myself." The clerk nodded while trying to restrain his smile. Tango had come to the Keys to talk to his old boss. Mr. DiNapoli was the only one he knew who could or would help him protect the future of his operation. There wasn't anybody better to hear it from than the man who'd started it all. Old Mr. D knew more about the Mafia boys and their operation than they did.

When he called the old man's phone and heard Tango's voice he said, "Hey you old rattlesnake what are you waking up the dead for? There's nothing left for you to take off me." Tango laughed as he visualized him sitting in a nicely padded, and well financed, tropical retreat. "Hey Mr. D. I know better than to try and take anything off your old slick ass. If I tried it I'd be the one who ended up with something missing. I just wanted to see what you were up to and talk about what's going on back home. Think we can get together for a minute?" DiNapoli still couldn't say no to Tango. "Now you know you're always welcome to see me anytime you feel like it Tango. When you're ready just drop on by. If you want I can send my man over there to pick you up." Tango wanted to drive his own car and said, "That's alright Mr. D., I can make it over there I just want to know if you want me to bring you anything." "I've got everything I need Tango, unless you've got a couple of sexy women you want to share." They both laughed and hung up. An hour later Tango pulled up to the old guy's ranch style beach house. He was shocked at how huge it was and how well the old man was living. The money from Tango's payoffs were keeping him in high style and luxury. The house was a few hundred feet from the beach, and had everything you could ask for. There was even a small boathouse down by the water. Tango walked up the tiled walkway and admired how neat and trimmed everything was. As he got closer the door opened and somebody looking like a linebacker filled up the frame. He had on some shorts and a tee shirt, but he probably would've been more comfortable in a helmet and shoulder pads. The gorilla led him as far as the living room and stopped. "Mr. DiNapoli is out back by the pool Mr. Mitchell, can I get you anything to drink?" Tango didn't even want to smell any more liquor. "Yeah, I'll take a tall glass of orange juice if it's not too much trouble." The guy nodded and sped off.

Tango walked to the back of the house and saw the old man. He was sitting in a motorized wheel chair with a huge Cuban cigar in his hand. He really was out there checking out the tight tanned beach bodies playing by the water. Tango pulled up one of the chairs arranged under the huge umbrella and got closer to the old dude. When he did, DiNapoli reached out and grabbed Tango's wrist. Tango tried to pull his arm away but he could tell the old man's grip was strong. Laughing Tango said, "Hey old man you been working out or something?" "I don't need to do that to keep you young kids in line." They both laughed and enjoyed a playful game of tug of war. The expression on DiNapoli's face turned serious when he asked, "So what brings you down to the mountain Tango?" Tango looked into the old man's eyes without cracking a smile. "I need your help Angelo. I think things are starting to turn against me there. I need you to let me know if there's any way I could make a clean break from the crew. I've done everything I agreed to when I took over your territory, but it seems like they don't want to respect that. I'm getting the feeling I need some kind of protection from their greedy ways. I'm planning on retiring soon, and I know they're going to try and split my territory up amongst themselves. You know I've already made arrangements with my family to pass things on to them. They've agreed to keep up all the agreements I made with you before you left. There's no reason for things to change, but you know how they are. I don't have to tell you why I need a backup plan. I have to make sure I can keep what's mine and protect my family from any problems the crew could cause." DiNapoli didn't react to what Tango said, he just rubbed his chin and grunted like he wanted to say something. "Tango the only way to protect yourself from greedy men is by threatening what they value."

"If you're serious about retiring, I'll help you do it. If you're not around, what about those payments I'm supposed to get? I know you'll make sure they keep coming, right?" Tango smiled and said, "If you help me keep my turf, I'll make sure those payments come for as long as you live. That's what we agreed to do isn't it?" DiNapoli nodded his head. "That's what you said, and I haven't had any reason to doubt your word. Now listen, if you want to really squeeze their balls, get your hands on one of their heroin shipments. When the shipment comes you grab it and hold it for ransom. After they agree to your demands, you can do whatever you want. What's good about that is, you keep them worried about their profits. They will never know what you might do next, right? When you give their dope back to them they'll understand you're a man of your word, but not to be fucked with." Tango didn't want to go against the old guys on the commission. They wouldn't get involved in local beefs unless it messed with their cash flow. Snatching a dope shipment messed with their cash flow big time. "Mr. D. the commission will rain holy hell on me if I blocked their hustle because of a beef with the crew. The only reason they went for me getting your turf was because you said it was your decision." DiNapoli shook his head and shrugged his shoulders. "You don't have to worry about those guys, they'll know what happened before the Bronx boys do. I'm going to make sure they know what the problem is and how it's getting fixed too alright?" Tango must have breathed a sigh of relief because DiNapoli grabbed his shoulder and shook him playfully. He liked the old man's plan, but still needed the right information. That's how he'd know when, where and how to pull it off. "But how am I supposed to get my hands on their dope shipment?" DiNapoli just smiled like the cat that ate the canary. "I've known all about their system for a long time. As long as you keep your word to me I'll lay out everything you need to know."

When Tango left DiNapoli's villa, he felt a lot better about the future of his business in the Bronx. Now he had a way to get out of running it every day. Now that he had the information and backing he needed to keep his turf secure, he could concentrate on who'd done that shit to Jazmyn. Knowing he had a plan in place, and the commission would be on his side, gave him a feeling of security. Those hungry jacks in the crew wouldn't be going crazy when they found out he had the backing of the commission. By the time he got back to his suite, the hangover was finally starting to wear off. Tango stripped off his clothes, lit one of the Cuban cigars DiNapoli had given him and stretched out in the huge Jacuzzi. He felt like the weight of the world had been lifted off his shoulders. The good news from DiNapoli had given him a new sense of freedom. He wanted to relax and let his mind go on a long overdue and much needed vacation. No matter what, he couldn't stop thinking about taking revenge on whoever killed Jazmyn. His mind wouldn't stop turning everything over and then turning it over again. If he couldn't find somebody to direct his anger at, it would be an ache in his gut. He couldn't get it out of his mind that she'd never used any kind of drugs. His mind settled into a cold and calculating mode as the turbulent water churned away the aches and pains his tired muscles were holding onto.

After about an hour in the Jacuzzi the hotel room phone rang. He picked it up wondering who could be calling his hotel room. "Hello, may I help you?" The woman's voice said, "Hmmmm, you sound very businesslike, I like that in a man. I hope I'm not disturbing you, I'm just checking to see if you're alright. After I left you this morning, I couldn't help wondering if you'd fallen into another bottle of rum and couldn't get out." Her sexy laughter didn't make the ribbing any more welcome. "Well if you were so concerned you should have acted like a bottle guard to make sure nothing like that ever happened again. If it had happened again it would be all your fault." She wasn't about to let him pin the blame on her. "If you need me to keep you from hurting yourself maybe you're not safe being left alone. Who knows, you might be trying to hurt yourself on purpose." Tango liked how she was coming at him, but he knew conversation wasn't what she was really after. "Well, now that you know my room number, you can decide for yourself whether I'm safe to be around. If you think it's safe you should come see about me." She laughed again and said, "I couldn't make a decision like that unless you invited me to your room." They both knew she already wanted to come. "Baby, if you don't know when you're being invited, you're not as smart as you look." This time when she laughed it sounded even sexier than before. "I'll be there in two shakes of a lambs tail, and I heard those things really know how to shake their tails!" Tango's mind was on some other kind of tail when he said, "I'm not that familiar with lambs, but I'll bet there's at least one woman that can give them a run for their money." She laughed a little at the joke, and said, "Umm hmmm" with a lot of sarcasm. "Yeah, I'll bet you do know something about that now don't you?" Click.

Kim Sanders was the type of girl always on the lookout for her next come up. She believed you made your own luck. She'd worked hard to make sure that her luck was always good. She'd run away from home because of an abusive mother and the promise of abuse from her mother's boyfriend when she'd only been 17. Their abuse had been too much for her to take. The streets were a risk too, but she didn't have any choice. That was six years ago, and since then she'd kept herself upright in the street by using nothing but her wits and the skills she picked up along the way. This was the first time she'd been on a vacation by herself. This was the only time she'd been away from New York without being somebody's guest. It felt a lot different coming and going as you pleased, without having to get anybody's permission or approval. Even though she felt bad that her man Jalen was sitting in a New York city jail, she didn't see why she should be in mourning. The way they'd snatched him up, it didn't look like he'd be getting out anytime soon. After his arrest, their business slowed way down. She took that as a sign for her to take some much needed time off. She decided to give herself a well deserved break. Running along the beach and finding an OG hadn't been on her schedule, but he looked like he was worth investing some time into. She called Tango when she got on the penthouse elevator, and all he had to say was, "Come on up, I've already been waiting a long time for you."

When the elevator doors slid open she was shocked at how much larger the penthouse suites were than her room. Yeah, this dude was definitely top shelf. She made up her mind right then she'd make sure, by the time she left, he'd think she was worth his time too. She walked in and flashed her sexiest smile at him. "You've been up here in all of this luxury waiting for me? I thought you'd be surrounded by all kinds of women trying to get your attention. I wonder what makes me special enough to get waited on?" Tango came out of the bathroom with his silk robe purposely left halfway open. He wanted to let her see the print of his meat. She needed to know there wasn't anything in between it and her but time and opportunity. The only thing keeping her from getting a full view were his matching silk pants. With a sly smile Tango said, "I've been waiting for you because I'm still curious about you. There's still a lot I haven't found out about you. I guess the not knowing part makes you exciting. You're also a little bit mysterious, when you're as old as I am, those things are pretty hard to find in a woman." Kim smiled as she nodded her head and sat down at the small dining table. "Well, I hope I'm a lot more than just a curiosity to you., Because you're already more than that to me. I came up here because I wanted to thank you in person for covering my hotel expenses. I also wanted you to know there's something about you that makes me feel something more than just a little thankful."

Right then there was a knock at the door. Tango opened it and the bellboy came in pushing a dinner cart loaded up with a complete surf and turf dinner for two. After the bellhop finished arranging the meal, Tango slipped him a crisp 50 and turned to Kim. "Dinner is served. I hope you don't mind me ordering for you. I just assumed from seeing your thick and healthy body that you were a meat eater." The smile he had made her think there was more to it than he meant for it to sound. She let him know there wasn't anything she wasn't prepared to do if that's what she felt like doing. "You know, I could eat almost anything if it tastes good. I also know that everything that tastes good ain't good for you. So, are you good for me?" With a mischievous half smile on his face he gave her a long slow look and said, "I don't know, but I've been told I taste pretty good." He had to laugh when she said, "Well if you're good for me, maybe we'll have to have a taste of each other." In her head she was saying, "If he wants to get some of this he's going to have to show me I'm not just another piece of ass he bagged. "So Tango tell me something, what are you doing down here in the sun and fun all by your-self? Did you get loose from the Mrs., or is she meeting you down here later?" He screwed up his face and said, "There isn't any Mrs. coming here for me. If I had one I wouldn't have been looking at you like a pit bull at a steak bone. I'm just down here to get away from the city. I needed to relax in the sand with nothing but good things on my mind. You happened to catch me in one of my drunken states. I decided to get myself together and see what I thought of you when my mind was right." She smiled at the compliment and said, "Well now that your mind is right, tell me what you think of what you see? Do you still want to find out about the mysterious woman? Because I have a few questions I'd like some answers to about you."

The time passed easily. They talked about a lot of different things and tested each other's limits on certain subjects. They enjoyed their time with each other, eating their dinner. In all that time, they never came close to what they both really wanted to know. When the dinner was done they talked about what they wanted for themselves and how they were going to get it. After they finished drinking the rest of the wine, Tango went over to the balcony door. He and opened it to feel the breeze and watch the waves of a beautiful ocean scene. It created a perfect frame for the moon, as the sound of surf outside had a rhythm like natural music. Tango wasn't feeling any pain when he sprawled across the cream colored chaise lounge and stretched out his legs until he was comfortable. He studied the motion of the ocean and let his mind take him places he never thought he'd get to go. Kim watched him make himself comfortable and decided to come sit on the floor next to him. She leaned on his thigh for support and lowered herself down. Tango felt like she just wanted to feel him up without being too obvious. When she leaned against him, she couldn't help but see the print of his dick start to rise against the silk pants. Unconsciously, she moved her hand to the front of his pants and began to gently rub and stroke the bulge growing there. Tango was completely relaxed, and Kim had decided she couldn't stop without seeing and feeling everything she'd already lived in her imagination. When she had fully awakened his serpent it had lengthened and swollen so much she had to push his legs aside. She raised up on her knees and moved over to what she wanted. He'd given her the invitation, and now she was taking everything that came with it.

Tango massaged her neck and shoulders as they both allowed nature to take its course. That's what made her feel she needed something hard and smooth in her mouth. She tugged on the drawstring on his pants to let her go where she wanted. Tango scooted back so his pants could slide down. She couldn't wait for what she wanted anymore. Impulsively Kim pulled his pants to get them out of her way. She took the rock hard shaft in her hands and slowly moved it from her mouth to her hand, up and down then back and forth. With a firm grip she gave the head a wet and sloppy kiss. All while she stroked the shaft back and forth, she slowly licked and kissed the head. The intense pleasure and sensual heat made her mouth water. It was juicy because she hungered for what was in her hands. She couldn't waste any more time, she slipped the head in her mouth and swallowed it. She licked and kissed it all with her tongue and lips. This was a taste she'd been wanting, and her tongue offered him a hot and slippery greeting. She started feeling like she had to be good to him, so her mouth knew how to treat a welcome guest. With each movement she fed more and more into her throat.

She was almost angry at herself for having so much fun, but she was too happy to suck on a big hard dick. Just sucking on it wasn't going to be enough. She wanted more. More than anything she wanted to feel it inside her body. Every time she licked or sucked, her mouth made her pussy wetter. She was ready to do whatever he wanted. She loved his hardness in her mouth. She took it in roughly, rubbing the head fast and hard against her lips. She loved the feeling of his head on her mouth, but it still wasn't enough. She couldn't take it like this anymore, she couldn't care what he thought of her. She wanted what she wanted. Kim opened her mouth wide, and stuck her tongue all the way out. Without thinking about anything she slapped his dick hard on her tongue. She loved it so much she rubbed it there back and forth. She didn't care about what he must have been thinking. This was what she liked it and it felt good doing it.

Tango stopped caring what she was doing to him. He'd given his body to her. She had taken control of him, and it felt so good he didn't care. She made him feel like his dick wasn't even his anymore. He squirmed and moaned from the way she handled his dick. He reacted instinctively to whatever she did. Her hands and mouth never stopped moving. She used her tongue and ran it all around his swollen head. She loved feeling him trying to restrain himself. It made her try even harder to take him past his self control. She was possessed by a passion for him that made her sexual nature rise. He wasn't letting her stop until they shared the best feeling they could. When he was about to burst in her mouth he let her know that she'd brought him to that point. All Kim wanted was to finish taking him where he had never been with her before. She wet her fingers in her mouth and used them to squeeze his head and shaft. It made him want to finish, but she wasn't ready for that. She wanted the reward to be nasty sweet. She loved the taste of cream, and wanted to feel it flow out like a river. When it came, it came all over her. It was all the way from his core. When she felt it she tasted it, and she loved it all at once. Then she gave in to the urge herself, she surrendered to it and released what had been growing inside her. What she needed to let out was there. It was hot and wet as it ran down her thighs. Like a dream she savored it. She licked his cum off her fingers, and surprised herself at how much she enjoyed tasting him. She was in her own world now. This was the kind of life she had always wanted to live. This was the how she'd always wanted it to be with a man. If she could make it flow, why couldn't she could eat as much as she wanted? So what if it dripped all over her, it was hers wasn't it?

When they'd finished, she stood up and sheepishly made her way to the bathroom. Tango's body tingled as he listened to water running in the bathroom. He couldn't help thinking, "What have I gotten myself into with this young girl?" This was the first sexual act he'd had with anyone not named Jazmyn for a very long time. Now that he'd let go with someone else, maybe he needed to realize something else. His woman was dead, but that didn't mean he had to die too. He was still going to catch who killed her and avenge her death. That's what his manhood demanded that he do, but his manhood also demanded that he live his life as a man. That's something Kim was more than capable of helping him do. When she came out of the bathroom, she walked over to where Tango was still laying back buck naked. With a soapy, hot wash cloth, Kim knelt down and carefully cleaned away the evidence of their nasty fun. She took her time gently cleaning off his body and lovingly caressing his limp dick.

When she was done all the traces of the DNA they'd shared was gone. She'd enjoyed wiping him down, and that's something she would have never believed she would ever enjoy doing again. She'd given him the kind of head she only gave a man after he'd earned it. That made her question what was going on with her. What had made her act that way so soon? Tango felt good knowing she was either already trained in how to serve a man, or could tell he was that kind of man. Maybe she was treating him that way so he wouldn't forget about her. Since she knew what she was supposed to do, he had to give her the proper respect. When she was finished cleaning him, Tango picked his pants up and put them back on.

He looked at the clothes she'd thrown on the floor, and at how she was sitting there naked, she looked like she was waiting for him to tell her what was next. "That was some thank you gift Kim, I see you know how to show your appreciation." He almost laughed at how she screwed her whole face up. "Don't you get this shit twisted Mr. Mitchell. I did not suck your dick to say no damn thank you. I just wanted you to know what you were missing by not having a good woman with you. See, I'm the kind of woman that knows how to take stress and tension off a man." When Tango saw he'd offended her he wished he hadn't said it. "Whoa, now hold up little lady, forgive me ok? I didn't mean any disrespect. I just thought we was cool enough to joke about things that's all. I didn't mean to offend you, I want us to always be good to each other no matter what ok?" She still looked like she had a hurt look on her face, but she got it together enough to make it sound like she was over it. "I accept your apology but I've really got to leave now. I wrote my number down and left it in your shaving kit. If we do see each other again, maybe you'll be thanking me." Tango just smiled, she was trying to let him know she wanted him to return the favor next time. Having a little bit of attitude made him like her even more. "Well I'll tell you one thing Kim, I can't wait until we see each other again. When we do, I hope you'll give me a reason to thank you." On her way over to the elevator, Tango noticed how she put a little extra twitch in her hips. She paused there for a second before pushing the button to open the door.

While Tango was gone Ellie really threw her weight around. This was the chance she'd been waiting for. She wanted to prove herself to Tango, and she wasn't letting this chance get away. She thought Tango had never given her the credit she deserved. This was her chance to show him what she could do. She wanted to show everybody she could run things on her own, but what she really wanted was to run things even better than Tango. When she found out he was gone, she started letting everybody know who was boss. She cut the crew at the afterhours bar in half on the weekends. That was so the payroll would be low and the club would make more money. She told all the dope houses to take more product if they wanted to pay the same prices. Since they weren't selling enough dope, it didn't justify them getting the low prices they'd been paying. She made them take 25% more dope if they wanted to pay their regular price. If they kept taking the same amount of dope, the price was going up 20%. She wanted to let them all know where they were on the food chain. If they didn't bring in more money, the dope was going to start costing them more. She started opening the club at 6 o clock instead of 10. She didn't want the girls hanging out in the bar unless they had a date with them, or were on the list for a date. She was trying to make sure everybody got their hustle on around there and was serious about getting things popping. She thought she was the only one who knew how to do it.

Meanwhile, Monica and Devon were getting into each other a little bit more than they should have been. Ellie was so busy running Tango's business, she didn't have time to keep an eye on them. Devon was trying to get used to being on his own. Monica made sure he didn't have many chances to be by himself. Everybody could see what was happening except them. Mike watched how they acted when they were together, and knew something was going on. But all he could do was shake his head about it. Ellie tried to keep up with her but the way Monica kept it moving that was almost impossible. She was doing so much and had so many places to be, she needed a social secretary. Ellie must have been feeling guilty about what she'd done to Jazmyn. Worry lines and dark rings were showing on her face. The dark circles under her eyes and new wrinkles were something no one had seen before. She was starting to look very old and worn out. Monica noticed how shaky she would act whenever they got near Jazmyn's apartment. She'd even started treating Devon like he was her responsibility or something. He noticed it and said something to Monica. "Yo Moni, what the fuck is up with your aunt? Man! She be acting like I need her to fucking burp me or something. Why don't you tell that bitch I'm damn near a grown ass man?" Monica snapped back, "Why don't you tell her your damn self, Mr. man! She don't do shit for me." The funny look on her face cracked Devon up. "Just tell me what you want her to do and I'll make her think it's for me." Monica didn't think it was funny, she pushed him and kicked his foot to try and trip him up. When he almost fell over she laughed. "That's why you almost fell on your face. I don't know what's wrong with her. She don't like nobody knowing where she be going neither. Notice when she goes out, she don't never want nobody going with her. She always be doing shit but not telling nobody what's up. All I know is she's a real sneaky bitch." Devon wasn't trying to hear about none of that, all he wanted her to do was leave him alone. "I don't care where she goes, she just need to stay her ass out of my business. Every time I look up she be asking me where I'm going or watching me when I come in. I can't wait to get out of here, so I can be somewhere of my own."

When Tango came back he was shocked at how much everything had been changed around. By the time Mike got him from the airport, he had seven messages from some of his best people. In the two weeks he'd been gone, his houses had complaints about things they never had before. They said his prices were too high, and they couldn't hold that much dope. They told him about having to buy more dope than they wanted just to keep their price down. Tango told them to hold on so he could find out what the problem was. He'd never had to say that before, and he didn't like saying it now. When Tango pulled up into the back of the building he was hot. Before he could even get out of the car, Ellie was on the phone. "I want to see you in my office as soon as you can get here." Ellie didn't know Tango was going be back this soon. When she found out he was back, she tried to get in a welcome back. All she got was dead air and a click. Tango had shut their conversation down because it meant she'd better hurry up. Then it was Mike's turn. "Alright Mike, why don't you tell me what's been going on around here since I've been gone. They sure ain't the way I left them, I want to know why not!" Mike already knew what was coming, and he wanted to make sure he didn't get caught in the blast radius. "Alright Tango, you know I do what I'm supposed to do around here.

All the houses been taking bigger loads or having to pay up more for them. If you want to know why or how, that's something you could take up with Ellie. Layla knows how the house's business has been getting handled, but all I know is they've been working longer and staying open more than before. Just try not to take it out on us. We were only doing what we're told to do, and as far as anybody knew the word was coming from you." Tango could see what position he was in, so he didn't bark on him for doing what he was told. "You're right Mike, I'll get everything straightened out and things will be back the way they're supposed to be. I just want to find out why things ever changed in the first place."

Mike got the suitcase out of the trunk and with a look of relief on his face headed up the stairs. Ellie could tell by the way Tango told her to come to the building she needed to be bringing him some good news. Her heart was pounding when she came in the front door. She brought that months books along with a bottle of X and O with her. She ran up the stairs, but waited for a second outside Tango's door. She wanted to get her breathing under control before she knocked. When Tango told her to come in, she saw him at his desk, and he wasn't looking too happy. That wasn't what she wanted to see. She'd been hoping that spending the time away would have put him in a better mood. Instead Tango's brooding expression looked like he'd gone on vacation and came back to nothing but a bunch of complaints. He sure wasn't looking relaxed or well rested. Ellie tried to start their meeting off by lightening the mood. "Well, hello there world traveler. I didn't think you'd be back for a while." Tango had a chill in his voice when he said, "Yeah, I know you didn't. Maybe that's why when I got back, everything was turned upside down. Who said I wanted anything changed? Who gave you permission or the authority to change anything around here? What made you think I wanted you to change anything? The way I was handling my business must have been ok with me. You'd better make me understand why I shouldn't run your ass up out of here. I can get somebody that knows how to stay in their lane and handle business the way I tell them to." Ellie was shook, and she knew this wasn't the time for any of her excuses. Tango wasn't trying to hear none of that bull shit. She figured the only out she had was to show him the increased profits. She pushed the account books to the front of the desk and said, "Look Tango, I know I should have waited on you, but you left me stuck here without me any instructions. I didn't know what you wanted me to do. Without you here to tell me how I was supposed to handle things I just took it on myself to do the best I could to make you more money. I just wanted you to come back to more money than you had when you left. I was trying to make things a little easier on you too. I know how hard you have to work to keep this going, I wanted to show you what I could do if you gave me a chance. Just check out the numbers in the books, we've been making you the kind of money you're supposed to get."

Tango sat there listening, but he wasn't impressed with any of it. "Listen Ellie, when I left, I thought I could at least trust you to keep things going the way they were until I got back. My business was operating just how I wanted it to be. I don't need you or anybody else to take over anything or make it into anything else. What you don't understand about business, is it's more important things are balanced and consistent. Consistency is what keeps things running smooth. Money comes because things are running on schedule. Problems come when something or someone throws that process out of order." Tango was looking through the books, and he saw that his profits had picked up. "There's been more profits this month, but these books don't show my unhappy clientele. They aren't showing all of the complaints that are going to make the relationships I've been building more difficult for me. How much time will it take for me to repair and maintain those relationships again?" He'd have to deal with a lot of hurt feelings and animosity because of her greedy experiment. "I see that you made a nice short term profit, but the way you did it turned my people off. That isn't doing me any good. Everything's going back to normal starting today. The club is going to go back to their regular hours and all of my houses are going back to their regular load quotas. They're going to get a 20% discount for the next two weeks. Because of you, I'm going to have to give them something extra to keep the peace. It's not easy to win back loyalty that never should have been questioned. But that's what I'm going to have to do." Ellie was disappointed and hurt, but she knew not to try and defend herself. Standing there looking at the floor she tried to make one more excuse. "Tango, I didn't mean to make trouble for you. I just thought it was better if you came back and didn't have to worry about anything. I wanted to show you I could handle your business if you ever needed me to. I was just trying to keep things going strong for you until you came back." Tango, still looking at the books in front of him, only looked up long enough to say, "Yeah Ellie I hear that, thanks but no thanks. From now on just help me when I ask for it. Tonight at the club, you can tell everybody I'm back. They're going back on schedule to the 10 to 10 shift." He looked back down before he said, "That's all for now, I'll let you know if there's anything else later on." Ellie nodded and mumbled "Alright Tango." before going out the door.

Later that night Tango came to the afterhours club to see what Ellie was doing in the office. Before he'd come back from his trip she'd been running sixteen hour shifts. He wanted to be sure things got put back on the right track. He could see that the drama and stress of the last three months was showing on her face. When he walked into the office without knocking she almost jumped out of her chair. "Damn man, you almost scared me to death. Don't you know there's a lot of fools running around out here? You can't be scaring people like that." Tango didn't bother reacting to her stupid remark, and that was almost as bad as if he had. She tried saying something fast since she could tell he wasn't there to play around. "What's got you out here tonight? You tired of sitting on top of the world already?" Tango replied in a dry tone, "Nah, I was at home thinking about how hard you've been working for me. I figured I should do something about that. You never say anything about wanting to take a break, so I came to tell you it's time you had a vacation." Ellie was stunned and surprised. She didn't know how to react so she just sat there. Tango waited to see her reaction, but when she just sat there he was disappointed. "Come on Ellie, say something. It ain't that big a shock is it? You *have* been on a vacation before, right? With all the drama that's been going on around here I figured you could use some time off. Everybody can't leave at the same time, so I figured you should be the first in line." In a sarcastic tone he said, "You don't have to worry about anything whi'le you're gone, I think can hold things down until you get back." Ellies mouth was opening and closing but no words were coming out of it. "I mean, uhhhh what do I ... I mean damn Tango, what am I supposed to do? How you gonna just come in here and drop some news like that on me? Like what you think, I'm supposed to be ready to fly out tonight or something?" Tango's expression looked like that wasn't his problem. "I don't care if you fly out tonight or walk out tomorrow, I'm telling you to get the hell up out of here. You know it's called a vacation for a reason, so vacate your ass up out of here before I change my mind. These premises are going to be right here when you get finished doing whatever the hell you're going to do."

The more Ellie thought about it, the more she liked the idea of taking a vacation. Going somewhere with none of the stress and worries she was used to did sound pretty good. "You know what Tango, you're right, this might be just what I need. I have been feeling kind of tired around here lately, but I knew you needed me. I kept it together because you've always had my back. Since you're ready to get back on your grind again I think I will get me some of that R and R." The smile on Tango's face wasn't a warm one, it was more of a grimace. "You deserve it, and after everything you've had to deal with lately, two weeks might not be long enough." Ellie didn't want him to think she couldn't hang so she said, "Naw, I'll be fresh as new money after I get through lounging around being waited on hand and foot." Tango stood there in the office waiting for her to leave until he had to say, "Ok, go on and have fun knocking yourself out. Everything will be right where it's supposed to be when you get back, I'll make sure of that." Ellie gathered up all of her things and cleared off the desk. As she was slipping her sneakers back on she said, "Oh yeah Tango, what about that work coming in Thursday? You'll have to check it out and weigh it up for Mike and Alphonso right?" Tango looked at Ellie with a scowl and said "Your ass is supposed to be on vacation right? Get on up out of here and let me handle this shit. I hope you have a good time getting your mind right, because by the time you get back I'll probably have everything screwed up for you." Even though Tango was smiling, his mind was on his next move and what it was going to be. He took out his wallet and handed Ellie his black American Express card. "You know how it goes. You can't leave home without it, and if it ain't black you ain't really going nowhere." Ellie took the card and said, "I got two whole weeks to do me and ain't got a clue where to start. Well wish me luck. I just hope I don't kill myself drinking." Tango's face kept its stoic expression. He pretended not to notice she'd mentioned something about death again. Ellie felt as low as a flea fart when she realized what she'd done, and suddenly got in an even bigger hurry to get out of there.

When she was gone Tango poured himself a triple shot of X and O, leaned back in his chair and had a long satisfying drink. He didn't have to think too much about what his next move was going to be. He'd been planning on making it for a while. He knew it was easy to push pieces into position, but if things didn't work out right it could be a bitch getting them back out. Ellie was gone so he sent a text to Layla: Wen U get a chance I wnt U 2 cum 2 da ofc. I nd 2 tlk 2 U. Hry up b4 I chng my mnd. A few seconds later he got one back: OMW. Tango didn't know if Layla was going to take the offer he had for her, but he knew she was a go getter, and had as much heart as any of the niggas he'd been around. She had never shown him any kind of disloyalty, and he knew you needed big balls to pass as much paper as she'd handled in her career. Layla had passed counterfeit bills, and had forgery skills that couldn't be beat. To top it all off she was known for having the gift of gab. She could talk to some of anybody when she was in the middle of pulling one of her frauds. Layla had connects with people who could create documentation and identification on demand. When Tango first met her he'd liked her. He could tell that she had game pumping through her veins, and always went full throttle because she didn't know any other way to get down. Tango knew he was going to have to keep a close eye on her, and that was where Mike was going to have to come in.

This was going to be Tango's big experiment, and it was either going to work, or blow up in his face. He just wanted to make sure he had enough back up around him to protect his operation from the aftershock. Tango heard an almost timid knock on the door. "Come in" Layla opened the door and just stood there waiting for Tango to tell her to come in. Tango laughed at her and said, "Come on in here girl and close the door, I've got some important business I need to talk over with you." Layla's expression took on a worried look like she was in some kind of trouble or something. Tango saw that and said, "First of all you've got to relax, you can't be around here acting all scurred. If you're going to be doing the kind of work I need you for you'll have to take charge." Tango smiled to try and get her to relax. She smiled back and he could tell some of the tension left because her shoulders relaxed a little. "Damn Tango, hell yeah I'm nervous. You ain't never called me up here for nothing before. I thought you was mad at me for something I did or I had messed up or something. Ain't I'm supposed to be nervous?" Tango had to laugh at her for thinking the worse before he said, "Layla, you've been doing a good job running the girls upstairs, and I know that's not easy to do. Couldn't I be letting you know that you're doing a good job?" Her attitude changed then and she started to look more confident. "Hell yeah I'm good at my job. They all know they better not act like they can't understand what I say. I'll put a foot in their ass and watch how quick shit gets real clear." Now this was the Layla he wanted to see.

As she was getting more comfortable in her chair, Tango wanted her to know what he had in store for her. "Listen Layla, I need somebody I can trust to run this whole operation for me for a while. Ellie's going to be gone and I figured you could handle it if I gave you the chance. She's taking a two week vacation right now but that ain't all there is to it. I need somebody to run things if I ever need to leave or if something comes up. Who knows, I might just feel like taking a break sometime." Layla couldn't believe he was going to give her that kind of chance. She was nervous, but excited about getting a chance to run the whole operation. Just being in the mix and proving she was a thorough bitch had gotten her the chance she'd been waiting for. Now all she had to do was prove herself. "Tango can't nobody else do what I can do for you. I'm going to work hard and always have your back. I know you're somebody I can count on and if you ever need me to do anything for you I'd do it because I know you'd do it for me." Tango nodded his head at her words and said, "I already know how you get down Layla, I know you're the kind of woman who likes being in charge of things. Wouldn't you like to take over this place one of these days? I've been watching you for a while now, and I see how you've got things going around here. I like the way you're always trying to do more, and you're the kind of woman who never stops trying to push things ahead. Now the question is can I get you to do that same thing around here for me? While Ellie's gone I'll show you everything you need to know to make sure things are flowing smooth. As long as the count keeps coming up correct we won't have any problems. Can you get with that or are you going to tell me you have something better to do?"

Layla couldn't wait for Tango to stop talking so she could

say, "Man, you know I'd love to take this job. But what's going to happen when Ellie comes back? Are you just going to send me back to running the hoes and doing the bookkeeping?" Tango could see even more why he'd liked her. She was already thinking and talking about what her future plans were going to be. She wanted to know what would happen when the probation period was over. With a sneaky sly smile on his face Tango said, "You're going to be my life jacket. If I ever need somebody to keep things from going under, I'm going to know I've got you somewhere close by. If anything happened and Ellie couldn't handle things, I'd have you here to take over. You're my insurance policy just like the Geico lizard. Only you're way cuter than his ass." They both laughed and Layla said, "That's cool, but I already know I'm cuter than that damn lizard. What I really want to do is to get paid better than his green ass. So what's my ends going to look like when I get through with the training?" Tango's eyes squinted down a little when he said, "Come on now Layla, you know I'm going to pay you for what you do. While you're training I'll pay you half as much as what Ellie makes, but when you're trained I'll pay you the same as what she makes as long as you're doing the whole job. If you aren't doing the job, don't expect to collect the pay. When you're not running things I'll still pay you more than you're making now." Layla was thinking about how good it all sounded and Tango knew it was too good of a deal to turn down. Right now it was a two week job that paid twice as much as her regular job, and it put her first in line for a promotion. "You know I'm going for this Tango. We both know how good you've been to me, and don't think anybody else has been trying to do anything good for me. You're the one who's always been in my corner from day one." Tango went over to the bar and picked up the bottle of X and O. " This seems like the proper way to kick off the beginning of a brand new day. Let's have a drink to get our new business off the ground the right way."

Now that Ellie was out of the way, Tango had to get busy getting the people in his dope houses straight. Once things were back where they were supposed to be, he started setting things up to make his move out of the game. That's what he was thinking about that morning when he came down the front stairs and saw Devon out there talking to Monica. He nodded his head at his two young charges. "Hey Moni, let me talk to Dee about something for a minute alright?" "That's cool Tango, I'll be upstairs if you need me Dee." She smiled, and when she left gave him a look like he was about to get a whipping or something. Tango laid his big paw on Devon's shoulder and said, "Hey Devon, I've been seeing you out here, and I can tell you like having nice things, right? You might think I'm not paying attention, but I can tell a lot from what I see. One thing I see is you ain't never hurting for cash. I know you don't have a job right? Whatever you're doing to get money now, there ain't nothing like having a steady income coming in. The only thing I'm telling you is it's always good to know when you've got that cash coming, how much and from where. I don't want you catching problems out here trying to get yourself paid. Just so you know, if you ever want a job you can always come and work for me alright?" Devon looked down at his feet and then down the street. "Yeah I know you'd look out for me Tango. I mean thanks a lot, but don't get me wrong, I know I need a job and everything, but my mind is still kind of shook up you know. With my mom being gone and everything I'm still kind of just floating by right now. I don't want to be the kind of nigga working for you that can't handle my business. I'd feel like a sucker for doing some shit like that. I just need a little more time to get myself together.

When I feel like I'm ready to be on my job, I'm going to come and ask you what you want me to do alright?" Tango grabbed Devon by his shoulder and in a low tone said, "Whenever you feel like you're ready just say the word. You know you're going to always have a place in the game with me. Just don't wait until you need a job before you get one, you know what I mean?" "Yeah Tango man, I got that. I'll be through to see you as soon as I think I'm ready." "Alright Devon, I'm waiting on you." Tango walked to the back, got in his Benz and rolled out.

Devon started out on a slow walk still thinking about what his next move was going to be. As he made his way down to the pool room he couldn't stop thinking about getting away from Tango's building. Talking with Tango made him feel like he was under surveillance or something. He needed to clear his head so he decided to kill a few hours playing nine ball. He could always win a few bucks off them fools in there. Snake and Chucky was posted up in back, as usual. Always holding down the back, perched up on empty tables, looking suspicious. But today, Devon saw things a whole new way. Things just didn't seem like they were supposed to be. For some reason his mind was stuck on Monica. It wasn't like it was just stuck straight on her, it's like it was stuck on her sideways. One minute he'd be thinking about working with Tango, and the next he was thinking about how Monica couldn't be his girl if he worked with Mike and Tango. When he thought about moving out of the building, he started wondering how he was going to be seeing her if he moved out? It had him puzzled but then he didn't mind it either. When something messed with his mind like that it usually made him feel like he was crazy, at least it did until he figured it out. But this time it was different, like this time he just had to take it. He didn't like how he was feeling, but he didn't want Monica to stay off his mind either. He was stuck like that, just hitting balls around the table and watching the people traffic come and go.

When he saw the way Keith came through the door, it was looking like he was in a hurry or something. As soon as he spotted Devon though, he left everybody else and came over there. He grabbed a stick of the rack and started shooting the cue ball around. Next he started a conversation saying, "Yo nigga, why your ass up in here lounging around? There's a whole world that's out there turning like a motherfucker." Devon walked around the table and stood next to him. He could tell by the way Keith was acting something was up with him. Devon had known him long enough to know when he smelled a rat. He wasn't coming down there looking for anybody unless he had to. That would only happen when and only when he needed your help. Keith would always want you to do the most dangerous part, then try to short you out of your share. Devon wasn't acting too eager to hear what he had to say. He lined up another ball and shot it. "My world turns wherever I'm at fool. Stop messing with my game and tell me what your ass is all amped up for?" Keith took a quick look around the pool room and almost whispered, "Man I got a shot up that's so tight I know we can both come up sweet. Plus we ain't got to worry about the police getting in it." Devon shot the ball closer and walked around the table. "What kind of move? I don't want to hear none of your fantasy bull shit either, keep it real nigga or keep it moving."

Keith was eager to share the details of his scheme. He knew without Devon to help him nothing could get done. Keith leaned in and got closer to Devon. He wanted to lay out his plan without anybody hearing him. "Man, I've got these niggas set up to buy a couple birds off me, but that ain't the deal. These niggas ain't even from here. If you rob us, we can have everything! When it's over me and you can split everything down the middle. I could buy your half of the dope with the money so you end up with all the money and I get all the dope."

Devon liked how it sounded, but he knew how Money was. Why would he be trying to make a deal that was so good for the both of them? Devon thought about it and said, "Point blank nigga, that all sounds real smooth, but if everything is over, how come you get to walk around like a victim, and I'm the bad guy? Yeah, it's all over for you. You get to be the innocent victim, meanwhile all the weight for robbing them falls on me. I'm the one that's taking all the risks. If I'm taking all the weight and risk I'm getting more than a fifty fifty split." Keith was pissed now, his plan wasn't going how he wanted it to go. But he stayed calm and still tried to sell it to Devon. "Yo cuz, this is my move. I'm the one putting everything together. I'm going to make sure they go along with it. You know you ain't going to have no trouble getting the money and dope." Devon knew Keith needed him, he couldn't trust none of the niggas in there to split the loot after it was done. If shit got too hot, he couldn't even trust their asses not to run their mouth about it. Devon let him know what it was going to be if he wanted to get down with him. "Yo nigga you'd better get your mind on the same page as me. I'm taking all the risk. All you've got to do is get robbed. When it's over, ain't nothing for you to worry about. Nobody's going to be looking for your ass. Ain't nobody going to be trying to find out if you was the one that made that move. When they lose their shit they're going to want somebody's ass to pay. In his head Devon figured up what the real count on the job would be and when he was done he let Keith know how it added up. "Listen cuz, we both know dope is worth more than money. Once that dope is sold the profit from it's going to come up to something real cute ain't it? For this shit to go down right, you've got to get down on it with a real nigga. We both know you need a nigga like me to get it on because you can trust me to take care of all that business. If you don't want to get down with me you can take a chance with one of these bum ass niggas in here. I bet you in a few hours they'll have your name in the street. It's on you to do what you do, but if you want to make this shit happen with me, this is how it's got to go down. I'm taking all the money and you can have half of the dope. I'll let you sell the other half of the dope for me and we can split the profits from that down the middle."

Keith knew he was stuck. Even though he felt like he was getting screwed, he didn't have any better options. He didn't have enough time to make anything else happen. If he tried, he wouldn't have enough time to pull it off. The buy was already set up. He had to go with whatever he could get. Keith really needed the dope so he could flip it, pay for what he'd already been fronted and then buy some more to keep his hustle going. The money wasn't his anyway, he wasn't really losing anything by giving that up. The dope was going to get turned over in a couple of days. After he'd stepped on it, Devon wouldn't know how much he'd really made off it. It only took him a few seconds to say, "Alright nigga, I guess it's got to go like that, but you know you doing me wrong." Devon didn't look like he gave a shit. "Man I ain't trying to hear none of that, I'm the only one trying to stay alive out here. You know this stick up shit is day to day. You ever heard of a stick up kid's retirement plan? So when and where is this is great robbery supposed to go down? Oh yeah, you better be ready to take one for the team too. If you really trying to to sell your stick up story you're gonna have to make that shit look for real you know?" "Yo nigga, I ain't trying to win no Oscar. They can't prove shit on me! I better not get a scratch on my ass." Devon didn't want to argue, but he knew how the game went. "Alright, but it's going to be hard as hell to sell a "hold up" story when you set the whole thing up. When they start looking for somebody to blame, it's real easy to blame you when you walk away without a scratch. Them niggas is going to want to check your pedigree." He didn't want to admit it, but he knew Devon was right. "Yeah well I'm going to tell you this nigga, if I've got to take stitches I'm getting me some of that dough." Devon just shrugged and said, "Yeah, alright. You can get five stacks if I have to crack your ass, but the rest of its mine." Keith just nodded his head in agreement. More than anything he nodded because the deal was going down. When he was about to leave he told Devon, "Get your gear and meet me up in Williamsburg. I'll be at the record store on Broadway around 8:30. I'll put you down on all the details then." Devon nodded his head, he couldn't stop thinking about how much his life was going to change.

Devon drove his Maxima around the block on Broadway. He had on a canary yellow LA Dodgers short set and a yellow MLB cap with some fresh white Ones. He pulled up at What A Burger and sat there eyeing the block. Devon saw Keith walking down the street he grabbed the gym bag out of the back seat and stood back in one of the doorways. The gym bag had his ratchet in it so he stood as close as he could to the building to stay out of sight. Keith was still walking his way but hadn't seen him yet. He was so busy talking to everybody he passed he never saw Devon. Devon waited until Keith was next to where he was and stepped out in front of him. When he saw Devon's outfit all he could say was, "Damn nigga, is that shit bright enough? They gonna get blinded by that shit." Devon just smirked and said, "I ain't trying to win no fashion show, and when they see the open end of this ratchet I bet they don't criticize it neither." Keith was looking worried and acting so shaky Devon had to tell him, "Yo if you can't keep your composure together I might have to pop your ass!" When he said that Keith's eyes popped open. He was looking like some kind of Sambo. Devon looked at his face and all he saw was straight panic. Keith was serious, "Yo kid, what the fuck is wrong with your ass? What the fuck is you talking about popping me for? I'm the one bringing your ass in to do this shit." Devon playfully bumped him with his shoulder and said, "Awwww nigga calm your ass down, I ain't really trying to plant none in you. I was just playing. What you need to do is relax. All you've got to do is stay loose. You ain't got to do nothing but sit still and get robbed. A lot of niggas do that shit everyday without no practice at all." Devon was smiling, but Keith's face looked like he was taking it all too serious. Keith tried to show Devon he was ready to stand up to the job. "Listen nigga, I ain't worried about nothing after we do this. Both of these niggas is from out of town. After we're done with them they're going to want all this shit be over with.

One of them is from Buffalo and the other one is from Rochester." Devon nodded his head and started feeling a little more comfortable. At least now he didn't have to be looking over his shoulder too much. Since neither one of them was from the city, they'll be glad they left out of the city with their nuts still attached. Devon laughed at the thought of some more tourists getting introduced to another reason not to love New York. "These niggas still don't know how it goes down in the 212. We're about to give their ass a tuition free course in the art of getting broke." Keith looked at his watch and said. "Yeah, well it's almost time. I've got to meet their ass down by the salt piles the city keeps for the snow plows and shit. Everybody's riding in my van while we take care of business. When it's all over I'll take them to their car so they can be out." Devon wanted to know where he fit into the plan. "Yeah, well where am I supposed to be? I can't jump out of the dark as soon as they get with you. I need to catch ya'll in the van together. It'll be easier to keep control of everybody in a small space. That way I can keep control of what's going on." Keith just wanted to have some say in how it was going to go. "Yeah ok, then you can pull up after we get back from the exchange. Just wait down by the river and when we come back you can push them back in the van. Tell them you're going to kill everybody if anybody makes a fucking sound." Devon didn't believe what was coming out of his mouth. This killer vibe was brand new for him and it didn't fit his pedigree at all. Devon just didn't want him to stop being a tough guy until after the job was finished. It was completely dark when they all met up. Devon was waiting around the corner so he could get a look at the two tourists. From where he was he could see Keith's van pull up next to the Monte Carlo SS. The two guys got in the back of Keith's van, and Devon followed behind them. As they rolled through the streets they were busy counting out money and getting a taste of the product. When they were satisfied everything was good Keith pulled into a parking lot at the Marcy projects. He parked his van all the way in the back of the lot, and tried to be as far out of the light as he could get. That's where they stopped so the buyers could cook the dope up and make sure it was pure.

Everybody patiently waited for the torch to heat the water in the little clear bottle. There was no reason to talk, this was the moment of truth. Either the dope was going to be good enough or there wouldn't be any deal. When the biggest guy scooped up some dope and threw in some baking soda they all knew what was at stake. When he saw the water boiling inside the bottle he poured the mixture in. After a few seconds it started boiling again and after about 30 seconds they saw an oily coating floating on the surface of the water. The guys spending money sat back and watched everything intently. When they saw the stuff form on the water they quickly poured in a little bit of the drinking water they had to cool it down. When that happened the cook bottle started to cool down and the stuff on the surface sank to the bottom. They turned the bottle and swirled it around. That cooled it even more until the water in the bottle got clear. When it did the dope hardened until it turned into a round white ball. When they stopped swirling it around the ball settled to the bottom. The big guy shook it, and when it hit the side of the bottle you could tell from the sound it was as hard as a marble. Before they could get it out of the bottle, there was a sudden explosion of glass that startled everybody. The driver's side window crashed in and bits of glass sprayed all over the inside of the van. At that moment, there was so much panic and shock, the only thing anybody saw was the huge chrome pistol being shoved into Keith's face. A muffled voice behind a mask said, "Get your ass back there with the rest of them!" Instead of doing what he was told Keith asked, "Yo man what's going on? What do you want?" Before he could say anything else the gun came down hard across his face. "I told your ass to get in the back. Move before I pop yo ass and keep doing what I'm doing." Keith held his bleeding head and stumbled to the back of the van. Jalen was still sitting in the passenger seat transfixed by the whole scene. "Get your ass back there too. I'm not going to repeat myself again." When Jalen and Keith were both in the back of the van Devon got in the driver's seat. He sat so he his back was to the windshield with both his eyes and his gun trained on everybody inside the van. Jalen tried to talk some sense into the guy. "Look man, can't we make some kind of deal here? We're all brothers, why can't everybody get something out of this?" The masked Devon said, "Yeah okay smart ass, here's the deal. You're gonna shut the fuck up and I'm gonna take all your shit. Now put all the dope and cash in my bag, and I want all of it too! Empty out your pockets and take off your jewelry too. In about five minutes Devon had taken everything he wanted from everybody. "Alright now, ya'll can get your clothes off, and I mean all of them. Put them up here in the front seat with me. Hurry the fuck up too, I ain't got all night for this bull shit." Nobody said anything. Their minds were going through every scenario they could imagine where they might have a chance to get the upper hand. Nobody could see how they had a chance to come out of there on top, so they reluctantly obeyed his commands. In a few minutes Devon went through the clothes as they put them up front still looking for more money and valuables. He didn't find anything, but he did get a couple of nice semi-automatic pistols. When he was finished taking what he wanted he threw their cell phones as far as he could and tossed their clothes out the broken window next to the van. Then Devon told them, "This is how it's gonna go, I'm getting out and walking away. If I see one of ya'll get out before I make it around the corner, I'm going to let my conscience be my guide and shoot until I get away. I ain't got no conscience so I hope you ain't counting on no shit like that to save your ass." Next he took the keys out of the ignition and threw them as hard as he could before he got out. Devon walked away with his stocking mask still covering his face. To him it was like Halloween or something. Even though he had the mask on people he passed hardly noticed. He smiled with devilish satisfaction as he got in his car and headed home.

When Devon got back to his apartment he took his time going through the loot. The Jalen kid's wallet was full of the best credit cards. He was wearing a Piaget "Possession" watch too. That shit was going to bring a lot when it got sold. The diamonds in it were so clear and bright he thought about keeping it for himself. But that thought only lasted for a second. Him wearing a watch like that would draw too much attention. In his line of work, the one thing he didn't need was extra attention. The Jalen kid had $2,000 in his pocket plus the $74,000 he was about to get for the dope sale. The two suckers together had almost $2,000 in their pockets, but they didn't have any credit cards. They did give up some pretty nice jewelry though. They didn't have anything as good as the watch, but one had a fat 36 in. platinum chain. The chain had a chunky pendant that must have gone with the white gold Rolex Presidential. There were a couple of fat diamond rings in the bag too. But the best thing was those two keys of raw yayo. Once some feet got put on it that stuff would be worth 5 times more. He knew Keith would be hot about getting smacked in his grill, but ain't nothing like some convincing scars to keep your ass from being under suspicion. Devon decided to give the watch to Tango. Nobody would question him about it or wonder where he got it from. That joint would look real official peeking out from under his cuff. Questions about how he could afford a gift like that was gonna have to wait. Devon was starting to feel good about being on his own, but he still missed his mom. Yeah, he liked being able to do whatever he wanted, but it was hard when everything in there reminded him of her. When Keith came to pick up his share, Devon knew he'd have to give him a little something extra for the lick he took. He didn't mean to smack the shit out of him like that, but sometimes you've got to take one for the team.

The next morning around 8 o clock, Devon woke up to Keith at his door with a big ass a gauze bandage over his left eye. It covered an ugly lump and about 8 fresh stitches. That shit was worth way more than the 5 G's he was about to get paid for it. He took the money, but the way he looked at it and back at Devon, he wished he'd asked for a lot more. "Yo nigga that was some real foul shit you did. Why you have to hit me that hard in my face?" Devon did feel a little bit sorry for what he'd done. "Come on man, you know I wasn't trying to do you like that. I guess my adrenaline was pumping when I hit you. I really ain't mean to clock you that hard though." Then Devon quickly changed the subject to something more pleasant. "But yo kid, check out all the loot we got. Come on now nigga, you know we came up! Check it, we got ratchets, credit cards, jewelry and shit. Yo you can take these credit cards and make a move with em if you want to, they ain't no good to me. Keith was still thinking about the bandage on his head. "Just throw them credit cards in the bag with that dope, I've got to put a few moves on it before I pass it off." Devon was only too happy to give that shit to him, the sooner it was away from him the better. Devon reached under the table and handed him the gym bag. "So how long is it gonna take you to move these two bitches?" What he really wanted to know was how soon he could get his half of the profit. Keith was too pissed about his head to be worried about a schedule. "Yo nigga, I ain't got no crystal ball. I'm turning one into powder and rocking the other one up. The powder moves slower but pays twice as much. I should be able to clear 50 G's off the one I turn into sniff and get about 30 stacks off the one I rock up.

That's gonna be like 40 apiece. Yo drop my money back on me from last night. You might as well sell my watch along with everything else. It would look kind of stupid for me to still have the watch I just got robbed for." Devon's face got real sour when he said that. "Yo check nigga, I ain't on that kind of mission. Don't be acting brand new, this ain't the kind of shit I do. I takes cash and pop niggas that can't take a joke. You can take these hot ass credit cards with you and your watch can go straight down to the pawn shop. I know it's some hypes in your crew that can max them credit cards out before it's too late." Keith wasn't in the mood to argue about any of that shit. All he wanted to do was get out and start turning that dope into some fresh pressed cash. He picked up the credit cards and said, "Yeah that's right Dee, I got some crack heads that'll go shopping and bring me everything they get for a few rocks." Devon smirked and said, "Just so you don't have they ass coming here looking for you." He laughed at his own joke while he dialed Monica's number.

Devon wanted to celebrate his most recent score and figured Monica would be some good company to do that with. He'd been letting her hide out in his spot whenever she didn't want to go to school. As long as she stayed out of sight nobody would know she was there. It was just like when he used to skip school in the pool room. She answered the phone sounding like she was still asleep. "Ummm Hello?" Trying to sound cheery and professional he said, "Good morning Miss, you're the first contestant on the Hot 97 Wake up and Win Show. May I ask who I'm speaking with?" Monica cleared her throat, "Uhhh yeah, this is Monica Hall." Holding in his laugh, Devon kept going. "Well Ms Hall, If you can answer these three simple questions correctly you'll be the winner of an all expense paid trip to Miami for Labor Day weekend. Do you think you'd like to try and win a prize like that?" Now she was wide awake. "Hell... I mean heck yes." "Alright then Miss Hall, see if you can tell me the first answer of the contest. Who's picture is on the fifty dollar bill?" Monica said, "Aww that's too easy. Ulysses S. Grant" "Oh that's right. Okay, I can see you're very familiar with money. So how about this one. Which U S president is on both coin and paper currency?" Monica was stumped for a minute and then she thought for a second and said, Ohhh Ohhhh Abraham Lincoln." Devon knew he had her going good then. The next question was the one he wanted to hook her with. "Alright now Miss Hall, if you answer this final contest question you'll be the winner of a fabulous trip to Miami along with your choice of any rental vehicle to drive for a week. Are you ready to answer the final question?" Monica was almost squealing now. She was breathing so fast it was hard to hear her when she said, "Ok yes I'm ready, come on what's the question?" Devon said, "The question Miss Hall is, Who do you know that would call you up and trick you in the morning for no reason like this?"

Devon held his breath trying not to laugh. He didn't want to tip her off or miss her reaction when she found out he was punking her. The phone was so quiet he thought she was still thinking over the question. He waited about 30 more seconds before he said, Miss Hall are you still there?" Monica said, "Yeah I'm still here. I'm just trying to understand what the last question was. I don't know that many people. Can you give me some more time?" By now Devon was dying from trying to hold his laughter inside. He got himself together and said, "Miss Hall I only have two minutes for the contest. If you can't answer in 60 seconds you're going to have to try to win another time." Monica said, "Well, can I just hear the question one more time please." The whole time they were on the phone Keith had been sitting there shaking his head back and forth. He didn't know which one of them was crazier, him for asking or her for answering them dumb ass questions. "Alright Miss Hall, the final minute starts now. Who do you know that would call you up and trick you like this in the morning for no reason?" When he finished saying it Monica threw a big bowl of ice cold water all over him. Devon jumped up from the couch, trying to recover from the shock of being soaked from head to toe with ice cold water. Keith was laughing until his head started hurting again. His head was killing him, but he couldn't stop staring at Monica's body. The way she was standing in the middle of the room, every one of her curves was on full display. All she had on was some skin tight Yankee shorts and an extra long white wife beater. What really had him stuck was the evil looking grin on her face. She was enjoying how she showed them she had power over them. "That's what you silly niggas get for playing kid games with me." The cold water had soaked Devon so bad he still hadn't recovered. What shocked him even more was how fine she looked. He pulled off the wet shirt and tried to get his thoughts back together. When he started feeling almost warm again he asked her, "How did your ass get in here like that?" She just curled up her top lip and said, "Nigga, you ain't know? I been had a key to this spot. Don't never think you're ahead of me in the game fool."

That was when she paid attention to Keith's head for the first time. When she looked at the bandage and his face, with a half laugh she screamed, "Dang!!! You got knocked the fuck out!!! Who did you fuck with that put they foot up in your ass? Somebody probably caught your ass trying to look in the wrong window or some other old creepy shit. Whatever it was they put a good one on your ass." She was smiling when she said it, but nobody thought she meant for it to sound nice. Keith didn't say anything about his injuries, and she didn't really care anyway. He hoped she'd just leave it like that. "Think whatever you want to think, it's probably still better than what really happened. I'm touched you're so concerned." Monica just smirked and turned her attention back to Devon, "You ain't got no business playing on my phone like that either nigga. The next time you try some shit like that I'm gonna come up in here with a pot of some steaming hot grits." He wasn't paying her crazy ass any attention, he was trying to get his wet clothes off. Who cared about what she was talking about anyway? When he came back out of his room with some dry clothes on, Devon got in her face. "That's the kind of dumb shit that shows you need to let me take some of that pressure off you. Your ass around here going straight crazy because ain't nobody tightened your ass up yet. I'm the only one with enough nerve to tell you about yourself." Monica struck a defiant pose and put her hand on her hip. With her lip turned all the way up she said, "It don't take no nerve to tell me anything, all it takes is somebody who's got enough pressure on their ass to be acting just as crazy as me." Devon had himself back together by then, and let her know he wasn't one of her suckers. "Whatever fool, but ain't nobody going to clean up all this mess you made in my floor." Monica turned her head and rolled her neck when she was walking away. "Hmmmmph You better make sure you wait on *that* nigga, cause I ain't cleaning up shit." Then she was out, just like she'd come in.

Things kept on going on the way they'd always been. There hadn't been a lot of changes, but if there were, everybody made adjustments and adapted to the way things were.

Keith was still trying to live out his fantasy, trying to be the man with the strongest game in the hood. After him and Devon quit running together, Keith went off on his own mission. He was all about making it big in the dope game, and that's the only hustle he wanted to be about. The dope game had everything he went for in it. He was always trying to move up, one way or the other. Money was willing to do whatever he had to do. He was ready to move in any and every way he could if it would put him in the game. The nigga loved everything about it. Handling the dope made him feel powerful because he liked controlling people. Having control of the dope meant it gave him power over what they did. Holding drugs gave him the upper hand on the weak and confused addicts he dealt with. In a way, he was as addicted to the power he had over them, as they were to the drugs and their addiction. His addiction was to making money and manipulating them. He got off on abusing the freaks and getting off on the hoes with his drugs. He knew they weren't attracted to him, but he still loved taking them through changes to see how far they'd go for that hit.

The only reason they did what he wanted was because of the dope. An addicted female would do any freak nasty thing he wanted as long as they could get that high. They did even more nasty things if they were trying to stay high. The drug fiends followed him everywhere. Keith had always wanted was to be his own boss. He kept telling his connect Jalen he was tired of having to always pay the high prices he got charged for dope. Jalen didn't care what he said, he told Keith if he wanted to get some good dope cheap, he would have to go get it in Miami. Keith decided if he had to give his money to somebody to hustle, why not go where he could pay less and get better dope? If he had his own dope he wouldn't have to turn the profits over to them. All it took was a ride to Miami, and he could get all the dope he wanted. He didn't see why he shouldn't make the trip. That was all he thought about while he was saving his cash and waiting. How long was he supposed to stay one of the little fish? He was tired of being small time. Keith figured it was time to make his own break. One day in March he scraped together all the money he could get his hands on and got on the road to Miami. The only thing on his mind was getting to Miami and buying as much raw cocaine as he could. In his dream he was coming back to New York city to be the man he always thought he should be. Nobody was going to tell him what he had to do anymore. He was psyched about the trip and didn't think of anything except what it meant for his hustle in the future. When he came back he was going to be his own boss. He wasn't going to have to wait for his plug to get back to him. He was going to be the plug. He would pay whatever they said to get his own stash. Making the long drive had been the hardest part. Once he got down to the MIA, the New York plates on a Cadillac STS drew a lot of attention, from both the hustlers and the police.

At first, Keith didn't know where to go or anybody who'd hook him up with the right people. He rode around looking for the right parts of town where he knew he'd see something that would tip him off. Even though he was lost, he was still exploring the different parts of the city. After he talked to some of the people on the street and asking them about getting some dope he began to get closer and closer to what he was looking for. After about four hours later and couple of wild goose chases, he got hooked up with this kid. Keith was rolling through the Overtown section when he saw this kid standing on the street in front of a package store. Keith knew what he was doing. After he watched him for a few minutes, he could tell the guy was hustling off some little packages of dope. Keith called him over to the car and said, "Hey man, I see you got your hustle going out here, I'm trying to get something myself, do you know where I can get my hands on some weight?" Jessie took a second to check him out before he said, "Yeah, I know somebody, but he ain't gonna do business with nobody he don't know like that. If I tell him I know you he might do it for me." Keith didn't care what he had to do to get with the plug. "Look man, I got the cash he wants so if he's trying to get that weight gone he's gonna have to meet people he don't know sometime." Jesse calculated what could be in it for him before he said, "Listen cuz, I ain't got enough money to get my hustle going so if you hit me with a quarter I'll get you in to see my man." Keith didn't have any other options and was running out of time. "Alright, I'll give you a piece of the package I get if you hook me up. But if the shit is trash ain't nothing gonna happen." That was all Jesse needed to hear. If he could get enough dope to get his own hustle going, he didn't mind introducing Keith to his plug. Jesse said, "I'll find out when I can hook you up with him and when things are ready I'll hit you back. You better not be playing no games with this dude because he'll split your wig if you come at him with anything sideways." Keith heard that. "Yo nigga, I ain't come all this way to play no games. I need to get some good dope and get back out of here in a few hours. I ain't got time to play games with you, him, or nobody else. Just hook me up and you'll get your own dope to hustle with." That got Jessie psyched. "You ain't got to worry about none of that, if you take care of me I'll take you straight to the man."

Keith went back to the hotel and waited for his phone to ring. It was after midnight when Jesse finally called. When they got together, Jesse took him over to Carol City. On their way over there Jesse told him the dope was straight raw, and Keith let him know he wasn't giving up no money until he checked out the dope and it was everything it was supposed to be. As soon as Keith saw how the place was laid out, he knew the Jamaican guy Peanut was who he wanted to deal with. He had his men around for security and the dope was raw and potent. Keith knew when he got back he was going to have the best dope in New York. Peanut wanted a customer that wasn't going to be in competition with his other customers. They agreed on a final price of $48,000 for a bird and a half. Keith knew better than to take that much money in there with him, and since he didn't trust Jesse's ass, he acted like he had to go get the money. Instead of doing anything on the honor system he told Peanut he wasn't bringing the money in until he'd seen the dope and checked everything out. All the Jesse kid wanted was four ounces of dope. After they took care of business Keith gave Jesse his piece and they were done. After Jesse got his dope, he was out like a porch light. Keith went straight back to the hotel to try and relax. But first he had to get the dope ready to travel. He had to keep it cool for the long ride up the coastline, so it had to be wrapped up and packed in ice in a cooler. Keith was both happy and nervous.

Keith sat down on the edge of the bed thinking about where he was, and how far he was about to go. He couldn't believe how easy it had been to make the power move of a lifetime. He'd gotten his hands on a kilo and a half of raw dope and it had only cost him $48,000. Once he got back home with it he could get started on the kind of life he'd been planning. Only Jesse didn't tell Keith one thing when they were getting the drug deal done, he forgot to mention that he was hot as hell. For the past week Jesse had been looking for a way to tell the DEA something to get them off of his back. He didn't want any heat from the hustlers in the town. If they found out he was a rat he wouldn't last long. The DEA had stuck him up in a case a few weeks earlier. They told him if he found them a bigger fish than his ass, they'd throw him back. As soon as he was finished hooking Keith up, he called the number on the back of the DEA card in his wallet. Jesse told them what hotel Keith was staying in, the license number and a complete description of his car. When Keith woke up a few hours later, he wasn't even hungry enough to eat. He thought his program was all together when he packed the trunk and pulled out of the city. He got right on the 95 North headed for New York city. What he didn't know was that the DEA was on him as soon as he left his hotel. Before he even turned on the cruise control the State Troopers were all over him.

Keith had no idea how far into the shit he'd fallen. He was felt so good about getting out of Miami, he didn't go to pieces when the flashing lights of Florida state troopers got behind him. He figured they were going by to pull over another car. When they stayed behind him he pulled over so they could give him a ticket for some bullshit. Probably because he had New York license plates. He wasn't worried about them searching the car, they couldn't have any idea what he was carrying. All he had to do was be calm and do everything they said. In a few minutes they'd write their ticket and give him a speech about nothing so they could get back to doing nothing. But when he saw both police come up on each side of his car he knew something wasn't right. The one on his side said, "Would you roll your window down please." Keith let the window down about two inches and said, "Excuse me officer, but is there some reason you stopped me?" The policeman said, "Yes there's a reason, let me see your license and proof of insurance and registration?" Keith said, "Yes sir, I have them right here." He looked in the glove compartment and took out the plastic envelope. He got his license out of his wallet and pushed them all through the slightly opened window. He could tell the trooper was aggravated by the glass being closed so much because he said, "Could you roll the window down the rest of the way? I need to be able to see in the vehicle." Keith tried to sound pleasant when he said, "It's rolled down far enough for you to get my license and registration. I don't need to open the window any more than it is right now." When he heard that the cop didn't sound so pleasant anymore. "Alright smart guy, how about you roll the window down right now or I'll arrest you for refusing the reasonable request of an officer. Maybe you'd like to experience some of our very fine jail accommodations."

By now he saw the trooper on the other side of the car, start nervously fidgeting with the service revolver in his hand. The first cop looked intently into the car and said, "Alright, we've talked to you long enough. Put your hands on the steering wheel and don't take them down, now you're under arrest." Keith didn't have any more choices, all he could do was unlock the door and get out with his hands on top of his head. After he was handcuffed, they put him in the back of their car while they searched his car. It didn't take long for them to find the bundles of cocaine in the cooler. They congratulated each other for doing what the snitch had told them to do. They laughed and gloated over their success all the way back to the lockup. Keith never stopped begging them to let him go. He even told them he'd go back and set up the people he'd bought the dope from if they let him go. They weren't buying any of his pleas for mercy. It wouldn't have mattered if he'd written them out on some tear stained stationary, they weren't interested. After he was locked up in the station house a few hours, he got a visit from a couple of fat and nasty DEA agents named Harvin and Jenkins.

They let him know right away they didn't really care what he had to say. All they wanted to know was what he could do for them in New York City. They let him know right away if he wasn't ready to wear wires and make drug buys for them using marked bills he was useless to them. If he wanted to get out of the toilet bowl he was in, he was going to have to be theirs all day every day. He had to do what they said whenever they said it. Keith was so afraid of going to jail he would have done almost anything to stay out. He couldn't let himself think about what being somebody's wife in there would be like. He was willing to do anything he had to do to get out of this nightmare. The one in charge was Agent Harvin, and it looked like his eyes twinkled when he said, "Look Hampton, the only way you can stay out of prison is by doing everything we say. If you don't do exactly what you're told I'm going to enjoy taking you to Rikers personally. Don't worry your pretty little head about making new friends, Once your'e settled in, I'll make sure and introduce you to all of the biggest and meanest pipe riders on your gallery." Keith's face looked like he swallowed a balloon when he said that. He started his begging in earnest then. "Officer Harvin, please give me a chance. I promise I'll listen to everything you tell me. You already know I'll do what you tell me to do. As long as I'm gonna be protected from whoever I send away, I swear I'll be the best snitch you ever had."

Before they turned him loose in Florida, Agent Harvin told Keith to report to Agent Harry Parris in their New York city office as soon as he got there. Keith was so happy they let him get out of there all he thought about was going home. Once he made it back to the city, Keith went right to his apartment and collapsed on the couch. His mind was filled with nothing, just a jumbled swirl of disconnected thoughts. He was consumed by fear and confusion, angry at himself for what he'd let himself get into. All he kept thinking was his future wasn't his anymore. He owed what was left of the rest of his life to the bullies with badges. There was nowhere in the world he could go that would be far enough for him to be out of their reach. It was like he had barbed wire tied around his balls, with the DEA holding onto the other end. Whenever their New York city office pulled, he had to jump. Whatever he did or didn't want to do wasn't up to him anymore.

When the first light of a new day touched his eyes he was awake. He stumbled into the bathroom and got under a blazing hot shower. He made it outside and to the train station in record time. When he stepped onto the train, he realized these would be his last moments as a free man. After the train ride he walked blindly down 10th street until he found himself standing there, studying the directory in the DEA building. When he saw where Parris's office was, he pushed the button and waited for the elevator to take him to the 12th floor. This elevator was taking him to the start of a new phase of life as their slave. When he walked up to the receptionist, she looked at him like he must have been lost or something. "May I help you?" Keith already had a bad attitude, and he let her know it when he said, "Yeah you can help me, I'm here to see agent Harry Parris. My name's not important. Just tell him I was sent here from Florida by an agent named Percy Harvin. He's supposed to be expecting me." She replied, "I'll check to see if he's in. You can have a seat in the waiting area." When he looked over to where she was pointing, and saw how it looked, he knew right then he wasn't going to be sitting in there. It looked like a fish bowl. Anybody walking through there could easily see who they had waiting for a chance to spill their guts. He wasn't about to make it that easy for them to recognize him as a rat.

He told the receptionist, "Listen, I'm not going to be waiting up in here. If Parris wants to talk to me, tell him he can reach me on my phone. Give me some paper so I can write my number down, and give me his phone number too. I'll just wait until he calls me and then we can hook up a time and a place to get together. If he doesn't get to me soon I'll call him." Keith wrote his number down and took the office card out of her hand. He got out of that building as fast as he could, and he wasn't planning on coming back in there unless it was in handcuffs. If Parris really wanted to talk to him he'd better memorize that phone number. It had been over a year since he'd gotten arrested in Florida. Only nothing had gotten any better for him when it came to his relationship with the Feds. Keith had done everything they wanted him to do, but nobody said anything about those charges in Florida getting taken off his neck. They had told him to get the charges thrown out, he had to cooperate. But when he cooperated, nothing happened.

Whenever they wanted him to wear a wire or make a drug buy, Parris always threatened him with jail. Sometimes he'd even tell Keith he could make up some new charges to stick on him if he wanted to. He enjoyed telling him it wouldn't take anything but a phone call to have him picked back up and put on a bus back to Florida. That was his favorite threat, having him thrown back in a Florida jail. Doing that kind of shit to Keith made him feel good. It made him feel good because he had the kind of power he'd always wanted. When he told Keith he could send him back to Florida just so he would have to stand in front of some judge he knew, Keith knew then he would never let him get out from under those charges. Keith took a lot of bullshit from the police, but he also used being their snitch to his advantage. Giving them certain people who weren't useful to him had a lot of benefits.

Keith started to use his connection to the cops to wipe out competitors and expand his territory. Nobody could stop him from taking over turf or getting more clout in the dope game anymore. If somebody wouldn't go along with whatever his plans were, or they wouldn't cooperate with what he wanted, all of a sudden they'd have police problems. Keith made it easy to get them caught holding dope or making a sale. The other dealers were blind to what was happening right in front of their face. Keith planted drugs in their cars, wore wires, made buys and even sold dope to them and then had them arrested. They had him buy dope with marked bills, but sometimes he'd have to improvise. Keith was willing to do anything to stay out of jail, and there wasn't anything he wouldn't do to get those Florida charges dropped. When he found out how easy it was to use the police to get what he wanted, he made the most of it.

When Devon called him about hooking him up with a weed connect, Keith saw another way he could try to put some distance between him and those drug charges. He knew Devon was a stick up kid, and even though they weren't hanging out anymore, they were still cool enough to get down on whatever could get them paid. They'd fallen out over how they got their hustle on, but things had never really changed between them. They still kept in touch and got together whenever they had to do what they wanted. One always knew where the other one was. If he could get Devon hung up in some kind of stick up beef, that would get him out of the way and make Monica available. Keith wanted another chance to push up on her fat ass. With Devon in jail, she wouldn't sit around by herself for too long. If Devon got so caught up he had to bust his guns, he could hand Parris an armed robber or maybe even a killer. They might think that has something worthwhile to exchange for the drug charges. He didn't know if it would be enough to get them off his ass, but it was worth a try. It didn't matter to him who they got, as long as it wasn't him. This whole dope game thing was getting too crazy for him anyway. If you weren't willing to get crazy too, it could end up eating you alive. The world just wasn't what it used to be anymore.

The main problem Keith had was he couldn't get the respect he wanted. Devon had always thought he was afraid to go all the way for what he wanted. But that wasn't Devon's problem, instead of being afraid, he pulled moves like he needed to do it to stay alive. Doing stick ups and getting the drop on people was like breathing for him. It stayed on his mind so much, it was like that's the only thing he really cared about. There was one job on his mind that he couldn't do by himself. The way he had it figured out, it would take three men. Him and Keith could make it happen, but it was still going to take another man. Devon was tired of waiting on Keith to grow some balls. He needed him to get out of the dope game. As long as he was worried about what some freaks and junkies wanted, he'd never be a hustler who could take care of things for himself. All he ever talked about was putting down power moves and having more clout than the other hustlers. If he was serious, he'd have to take the chances real players took. Devon was ready to put in some work on that job he'd been lining up. He hit Keith on his jack. "Hey nigga, why don't you to meet up with me down at the bar. I got something I want to put you down on. Slide through and see me so we can chop it up." Devon almost hung up before Keith said, "Yo that's cool, but I'm gonna need you to help me out with some stuff I got going on, it's real easy. All I need you to do is back me up, I'll put you down when we kick it." Click.

Devon knew he wasn't handling no dope, so if that's what he had in mind he'd better think of something else. Devon had spent a lot of time hanging out around the stores down on Delancey and Orchard. He'd noticed how there were bigger crowds down there lately. Devon stayed looking for somewhere new to put down a move. His hustle mind was wondering how he could make something happen with that. Whenever he was over there buying gear, he noticed the Jews kept a lot of cash on hand. He hadn't pulled a good stick up in Manhattan. It was about the only borough he hadn't gotten a piece of yet. They handled more money on the weekends, and he figured it was because of the bus tours that came from out of town. His hands itched at the thought of getting his hands on that cash. A bus full of tourists with a whole lot of cash sounded like the kind of job that was meant for him. They only came through on the weekends, and just stayed long enough to shop. That meant they had lot of cash on them. If you spent cash with the Jews, they'd cut their prices and make deals. They didn't give sales receipts because that kept the sales tax off the books. They didn't have to report the money they made as income if they didn't give receipts. Nobody had a sales record so it was no proof they ever did any business.

Devon had been thinking about that bus full of money for almost three weeks. It was time for him to make it his. He'd been sitting in the bar over an hour waiting on Keith. Just when he was about to call him again his ass showed up acting like he was somebody important. He was so loud, Devon had to pull him back by the bathroom so they could talk in private. "Yo Money, why don't your ass chill sometimes? I got a move set up that's going to make your Christmas bright. Check it, we're going to knock off a shopping trip bus and get straight paid." Keith would have loved some extra cash, but a stick up wasn't how he wanted to do it. When he heard tour bus, he didn't even think about it. "Man you've got to be crazy, ain't nobody going to sit there and let you take all their money. You're talking about robbing a whole bus load of people. That's way too many niggas to keep control of." Devon wasn't giving up on it. "That's why I need you dude, if I could do it by myself I would have done it already. All you've got to do is keep the bus driver in his seat and make sure don't nobody do nothing stupid. I'll be doing all the robbing, when it's over with we'll both be out. Once we get away from the bus it'll be a wrap. They won't know what to do or where to go after that. By the time they figure out what move to make we'll be at home, straight paid like a motherfucker."

Keith wasn't feeling it. "Listen to me one more time nigga, I ain't about to be all up in front of nobody's bus holding a ratchet on the driver. Man, a bus got a big ass windshield on it. Anybody walking by could see my face and I D me. You'll be in the back of the bus, out of sight like it's alright. Won't nobody be able to recognize your ass once you get back on the street." Devon could tell he was scared. He heard the fear in his voice. He still tried to convince him. "Yo, Money I don't care, we could switch places. If you want to stick up the customers, you can be in the back of the bus. I didn't think you wanted to do nothing like that, you're always acting like you don't want to pop nobody. You know how shit be getting sometime." Keith thought this was a chance to get Devon caught up in a stick up so he'd have to shoot somebody. But he didn't see how he could that work. How was he supposed to get Devon in the right position for that by doing this robbery. The whole situation looked like a nightmare waiting to happen.

As Devon talked about what he had to do, Keith kept on looking all around the whole bar. He was trying to give Devon a hint that he'd lost interest in the conversation, but Devon wasn't buying it. At least not yet anyway. "Look man, me and you been down on all kinds of moves. This is one time I really need somebody down with me I can trust. I need somebody with me that I know is going to keep it together. Plus, I know you won't flip on me if things go down the wrong way. If we have to sit it down for a minute, I know you won't flip on me. It ain't but a few niggas who could stay true out here. You know I don't trust the niggas I run with like that." Keith still shook his head. "Look Dee, man you know I ain't no stick up kid. That stick up profile is your thing. When you pick up a gun you're taking your own life in your hands. If you kill anybody on that bus you're going to prison for the rest of your life. They ain't got nothing on that bus worth me giving up my life for it."

Finally, the truth started getting through to Devon, Keith wasn't really down with him. "Alright man, I guess if you ain't all the way down you shouldn't be in it." Keith was still listening but he looked like he was just waiting for Devon to stop talking. Then Devon had an idea. "Yo, since you won't get on the bus with me, you could drive the getaway car. That way you won't even be on the same street. All you've got to do is park somewhere close by. When I come around the corner and get up in the whip, all you've got to do is get us out of there. I know you can do some simple shit like that right?" In spite of the worried look on Keith's face, he said, "As long as all I've got to do is drive you away, I'll do it. But I'm telling you, I'll be far away from what you got going on. Won't no witnesses be seeing my face or taking down my tags." Devon was quick to tell him, "Man relax with all that, when I get to where you're at, it problems won't be coming from nowhere. Nobody's gonna know where I went after I get off the bus. Just make sure you're where you're supposed to be. If we keep that straight we'll both be out."

Keith said yes even though he wasn't all the way in on the job. He just needed the cash, and more than that he wanted Devon to be in his debt. "Man, I'm down to drive you up out of there. But if I see you getting chased or some other dumb shit, don't think I won't jump up out that whip and you can be on your own." Devon shook his head as he thought about how fearful Keith had become. "That's alright with me nigga, if that's the way you want to be then it is what it is. Ain't nothing like that happening anyway. When I get the last piece of this puzzle together I'll let you know when we're making the move. Devon was glad Keith would be doing the driving. He was scared, the most important part of any robbery was getting home with the dough. If you didn't do that nothing else mattered. He still couldn't believe how scared he was acting after everything they'd done together.

"Man I swear this is the one right here. Once it's over everything is going to be sweet as ever." Devon still had to make sure Keith stayed locked in on the job. He was acting so shady he figured if he made more money that it would make him more eager to take the job. "Yo man, I'm going to still cut you in for a whole share of the loot, that's the least I could do after all the shit we've been through together." Keith smiled and nodded his head when he heard he was getting a full share, but that by itself still wasn't enough to get his heart into it. He was strictly a mercenary, and this was all about the money for him. Quickly Keith drained his drink and said, "Let me know when you're ready to do that thing and I'll get up with you on it."

Devon was stuck because he knew he still needed another man to get on the bus with him. One man wouldn't be enough to control the driver and all of those people. He didn't like that Keith was too scared to get down with him, but if pulling stick ups wasn't in him he shouldn't be there. It pissed him off how he said no without even thinking about it. Keith knew he needed him right then, but that didn't make him any difference. He'd still left him hanging. Devon couldn't figure out why Keith was still trying to act like they was down the same as they used to be. All Keith talked about was how he couldn't deal with holding a gun on nobody. But he didn't have a problem selling them all the dope they could pay for. One death was quicker than the other, but they were still gonna end up just as dead.

None of the robberies Devon had done had gotten anybody shot, yet. Why was Keith so worried about it? Devon had to face the facts, Keith just wasn't down with him when he needed him the most. That meant he really wasn't down with him at all. For the next few weeks Devon hung around Canal street and Chinatown hard. He checked out the bus trip details and tried to find out what schedule they worked on. He wanted to know what time they arrived and where the passengers got off and on. Devon talked to some of the girls who were shopping, he found out a lot of the buses came from Buffalo. They left from Jersey around 6pm to get back home by midnight. They came to the city first thing in the morning but only stayed long enough to shop for the day. He needed another man, but he wasn't letting them hungry niggas from around the way know about it. They would've probably tried to beat him to it and fuck the whole program up.

Devon needed somebody who wasn't already deep in the stick up game, but still had enough balls to do it. Keeping the bus under control was the most important part and that was easy once they seen that ratchet in their face. Devon knew he couldn't trust none of them niggas around the pool room. Instead of wasting more time, he broke down and told Monica's brother what was up. When he told Mike he got so psyched he wanted to hit the bus right then. Nothing was happening until they knew the plan Devon had laid out. Keith was parking or waiting around the corner. Mike had to meet him after the stick up and they'd ride over to Brooklyn. They had to meet Devon when he got off the train and pick him up on Delancey street. From there, they'd have to get back to the hood. After being at Devon's drinking beers and going over details, everybody knew what to do. The Friday before the job they met at Devon's to be sure they were ready. Around 7:30 am everybody was tense. Mike and Devon headed downtown and got there about 8:00. The bus wasn't there yet, so instead of just standing around waiting, they separated and walked around in different directions so it wouldn't look like they were together. They didn't get out of each other's sight, but as the time crept by their nerves got wound up tighter and tighter. Devon fought all the negative ideas in his head and tried to stay focused on the job. Mike had him worried, he didn't like the way Mike was staring off into space. He couldn't let that or anything else keep him from taking care of his business. It was almost 8:30 now, and the bus should have been there. Devon pulled Mike into one of the bus shelters. "Listen man, don't let nothing stop you from getting that loot back to the van. I'll keep the bus locked down until you're all the way around the corner. Just walk fast and don't start running like no fucking wild man alright?" The way he looked back at Devon made him look like a zombie. Devon didn't like it, but it was too late to worry about it. All Mike said was, "You do your job and I'll do mine. I know how to handle this. I've been making moves like this a long time. All you've got to do is back me up. When we get on the bus just follow my lead and go along with whatever I do." Devon just nodded his head, this wasn't the time to start arguing about anything he couldn't control. It was too late to turn back, and when he saw the imprint of the pistol through Mike's jacket he knew they were going to have to take it all the way. He definitely didn't like him holding it in his hand while they stood there waiting on the bus.

The D&F Travel Bus made it to Manhattan and the McDonough street stop at 8:45 am. It stopped right behind the warehouses where Mike and Devon were waiting. As soon as the bus driver swung the door open Devon ran in and pushed the people back onto the bus, he showed the driver a close up view of his ratchet and made everybody standing there pay attention to his gun. Mike ran up the steps behind him pushing people out of his way as he went. Devon told the driver, "Shut the door back and don't do nothing unless I tell you to do it." Mike pushed past all the shocked passengers and plowed his way down the crowded aisle. Going down the aisle he held his chrome plated 9mm over his head. "Everybody sit down and shut up! You know what this is! Put your hands on the back of the seat in front of you! I don't want to see nobody making no kind of moves!" He held the pistol up high enough to make sure everybody saw it. As Mike was going to the back of the bus Devon screamed out "Everybody stay in your seat and keep your hands on top of the seat in front of you." The driver was shaking all over and looking from side to side like some kind of caged rat. Devon figured he needed to remind him who was in charge, so he smacked him on the side of his head with the barrel of the gun. "Listen up fool, long as you sit still and keep quiet everything will be over in a minute." By now Mike had made it to the last row of seats. He pulled a pillow case out of his backpack and yelled out instructions. "Take off all your jewelry, I want chains, rings, earrings, watches and bracelets too. When I get to your seat take it all off and drop it in the bag, when I get to your seat I want every wallet and purse in that seat. If I'm not at your seat your hands should be on the seat in front of you." As he went from seat to seat emptying purses and taking wallets Devon thought he was moving too slow. As each second passed Devon got more tense.

Mike cracked one guy in the back of the head hard with the gun butt. When everybody saw the blood dripping they paid a lot more attention. Mike had to tell him, "That's what you get for acting like you're running this. Who else think they don't have to do what I say?" It seemed like he was bugging but things were still going along pretty smooth. "When I say something I'm not saying it twice." The closer he got to the front of the bus the more violent Mike got. When he was almost done this fat nigga told him, "Look man, I ain't got no money on me. My wife is meeting her aunt down here, she's spending the money." Mike wasn't trying to hear that. "So you want to be a funny motherfucker right? Get your damn clothes off and give all of them to me." The man stood in the aisle taking off his clothes as Mike kept on taking the money and credit cards from each set of seats.

When the guy's clothes were off Mike said, "Yo nigga get your draws off too, I want your ass all the way naked." While he was covering up his crotch, Mike looked through the clothes on the floor. It only took him a few seconds to find a stack of hundreds in one of his socks. Mike drew back like he was about to pistol whip the frightened rider. But instead he balled the clothes up and stuck them under his arm. Next he tied the man's sneakers together and hung them around his neck. When he was finished Mike said, "See if her aunt can buy your fat ass a new outfit." It seemed like an hour had passed by the time Mike made it to the front of the bus. It had really only taken twenty three minutes, but to Devon it had felt like it forever. Judging by the looks on all the riders faces, it had been even longer for them. Everybody was looking disgusted and angry, but nobody made a move or challenged anything they said. It was time to go when Mike collected the last of the loot from the passengers in the front of the bus. He stuffed the loaded pillow case in the book bag and slipped past Devon.

Once he got on the street, Mike put the back pack on his back and quickly walked up Canal street. When he turned the corner, Mike saw Keith's van sitting right where it was supposed to be. Keith had been nervous waiting, but now that Mike was there, it meant that part of the job was over. The way Mike was sweating he didn't need him to say, "Let's get the fuck out of here, Devon's gonna have to take care of the rest of this by himself." Devon was on the bus by himself, and it seemed like the looks on the passengers faces got even more threatening. The only thing everybody watched was the gun in his hand. Nobody wanted to see him use it. The driver had a black and blue bruise forming across his right eye, but other than that he wasn't in bad shape. After Mike got off the bus there was a tense silence. Devon broke it by saying, "Alright, everybody keep your eyes on me. I don't want to see anybody's head turned around. This will all be over in a minute, as long as nobody does anything stupid."

It looked like a freeze frame from an episode of Law and Order for a second. Devon almost felt sorry for them, but that wasn't going to do them any good. He kept his focus on the main thing. Too bad this was going to be the lasting memory they had of shopping in New York. He stood in the doorway of the bus with his pistol trained on everybody wishing he was already around the corner. When he saw Mike go around the corner of Canal Street he yelled out, "I hope nobody tries to be a hero today. I'm getting off here, and ya'll can see another tomorrow." He jumped off the bus with his ratchet in his hand, before sticking it in his jacket. Without waiting, Devon turned and walked as fast as he could without running. Walking away he looked back, like he was waiting for somebody. If anybody had gotten off the bus and started yelling for help he would have been screwed. He tucked the nickel plated 38 down the front of his pants and covered it with his jacket. As soon as he turned the corner he started running.

He ducked into the first subway station and made it down

the stairs as quick as he could. He wasn't stopping to buy a ticket, he jumped the turnstiles and ran out to get on the loading platform. Once he was around other people he felt better. He hated standing around all those people, but he tried his best to look normal. On his way to the F train he spotted a garbage can, after a quick look around he pushed the pistol inside and let it go. It was almost 9:30, the terminal was starting to be less crowded. He had a weird feeling that everybody was looking at him. It was too late to worry about that, so he wiped it out of his mind. He concentrated on how happy he was he got off that bus in one piece. Now all he wanted to see was the uptown train. The cool breeze blowing through the tunnel was like a welcome sign telling him everything was going to be alright.

When the train finally stopped he couldn't wait for the doors to open. When they opened he jumped inside and stood up against the back wall of the car. The ride uptown was a mixture of tension and muffled joy. He was happy to be away from the bus and those people, but he knew he still couldn't relax, yet. Things always had a way of coming back on you without any warning. It's always better not to relax until you're all the way home. When Devon got off at the Essex Street station he breathed a little easier. He ran off the train and dashed up the stairs as fast as he could. He couldn't wait to get on the street so he could try to catch a signal. As soon as he had bars he called Keith and told him to meet him on the corner of Delancey and Orchard.

He walked as fast as he could, but he didn't want to look like he was in a hurry. He wanted to get there before them so he wouldn't be standing out there waiting. He tried to walk fast, but he felt like he was in one of those dreams where it feels like you've got weights on your feet or you're being sucked into the concrete. Everything had gone down like they planned, but they hadn't made it back safe yet. He felt like people were staring at him, but as long as nobody made a move he didn't give a damn. He'd gotten rid of the gun, and he didn't have none of the loot on him. Until he got in Keith's van, he could play innocent. If he got caught in there with the guns and loot, nobody would have a chance in France of getting out of it. If the cops got them before they made it to the Bronx they'd all be done. When he saw Keith's green Dodge Caravan turn the corner Devon let out a sigh of relief. When the van finally stopped, Devon jumped in and let out a yell. "Woooooooooo!!!!!! Man that shit was crucial!" Devon looked at the both of them to see what their attitude was like. Mike's eyes were popped open like he'd just sniffed a bunch of yayo and Keith was looking more nervous than either one of them. He hadn't done a anything and he looked the guiltiest.

Devon had to ask Mike about the dude he hit in the head. He had the man bleeding all over the bus. "Yo Mike, why'd you crack that kid's head open back there? I thought you was getting ready to go crazy." Mike thought about it for a second and laughed. "Oh, I had to knock some sense into his ass. If I would have let his ass go, we might have had a whole bus full of fools to deal with. You got to let niggas know you ain't playing when you're trying to get your money, ya know what I mean?" "You ain't never lied, we got paid lovely out of that." Devon laughed out loud and slapped Mike up. Keith didn't say anything. The whole ride all he did was keep looking in the rearview mirror. He was acting like he was sorry he came with them. Then Mike said, "Yooooo, the fool with the cash in his socks was the icing on the cake." "Yeah that shit was crazy. I couldn't believe you made him strip down to nothing. You ain't have to take his clothes and sneakers too. All I could do was shake my head at that." Keith acted like he didn't want to hear about what happened on the bus. He kept letting out long sighs and shaking his head. Mike remembered something else. "You see that old nigga in the red Kangol trying to act tough? I was getting ready to give his ass hot one for free. He better be glad his woman made him sit his old ass down."

Devon had to let him know about how slow he was moving. "Man you was coming down the aisle so slow, you must have thought you was Bob Barker. You ain't got to get every dollar when you trying to make time. Sometime you just need to leave some shit behind." Devon laughed at Mike's face when he said that. "Nigga, we was on there to get ALL the money and that's what I was doing. If you wanted me to leave some of yours behind you should've told me." Devon wasn't with that. "Nigga you wasn't leaving nothing behind, and if you did it wasn't going to be none of mine." Devon was having a good time until he looked at Keith. The way he was looking made him instantly nervous. "Yo Money, you alright? You need to lighten the fuck up. We're out of that shit now, from here on out everything's going to be nice and breezy."

Devon wasn't telling him what would happen if the police caught up with their asses right now. With all the evidence from the robbery in his van, the bag on the floor was enough to put them all in jail for a hundred years. Robbing each of those passengers was a separate armed robbery charge. Keith still didn't say a word, he just kept maneuvering through traffic, driving like they were getting chased. Devon looked at how the book bag was bulging. "Yo Mike, what did you do with that fools clothes? After you took the money out the sock you could've at least gave him his clothes back." Mike smirked him and said, "Fuck him. He ain't know? You should never bullshit a bullshitter. I threw that wack shit in the garbage as soon as I got around the corner. Now his naked ass can be the comic relief on there." Devon shook his head. "I bet he don't pull no shit like that no more."

All they wanted was to get back home and get away from all that evidence. The sooner they got home the better. Mike was sweating like he was going to the electric chair. They all wanted to make it back to the hood so they could relax. Nobody was safe until they were off the street and back in the house. As soon as Keith got in front of the building, Devon grabbed the book bag and rushed up the stairs. Once they all were inside, they could let the pressure off. Devon pushed the coffee table aside and poured everything out on the floor. Mike got some beers out of the refrigerator and Keith sat down on the couch. He looked at the pile of loot on the floor, and shook his head. While Mike and Devon sorted through everything, he finally spoke. "That's a lot of money and shit right there. Man, the police are going to be on a mission behind all this shit coming up missing."

Devon almost smirked when he said, "Yo, the police ain't got a clue about where this shit is. What do you think they know, on a Saturday morning? Where did a bunch of out of towners cash and jewelry go? They wouldn't even know where to start looking. All of its right here, but nobody's telling them that." Devon looked at Mike sorting through the jewelry and said, "It ain't nothing but a day's pay for a couple of hard working niggas like us." He meant it just like it sounded too. It had really been just the two of them that made it happen. Keith could have been a cab for all the good he was. Devon had wanted Keith to be down with him. He'd been his day one hustling partner, but now the was seeing how much bitch he had in him, and Devon couldn't respect that. He didn't like having to admit that to himself, but he couldn't deny it. He was seeing it for himself. With all the history they had, it would never sit right with him that Keith wouldn't go on the bus. He used to think he could depend on Keith, but now he knew for sure that he couldn't. Keith didn't act like he was really down for the hustle anymore.

All Keith thought about was making dope moves and getting with some nasty bitches. He loved freaking with the hood rats the drugs attracted to him. Devon and Mike high fived each other again while looking through all the dough spread out on the floor. When it was all sorted out they had stacks of cash in piles of hundreds, fifties, twenties and tens. They threw the fives and ones in the bag by the couch, those were Devon's. They put chains and rings in one pile, and the earrings, bracelets and watches in another. They'd have to use the credit cards fast, it wouldn't be long before they'd be too hot to use. It wouldn't be safe to move the jewelry until things cooled down. The most important thing was counting and splitting up the cash. Devon picked up the pile of hundreds and dealt them out one like playing cards. He put the last two bills left to the side. Next he did the fifties, the twenties and finally the tens. When he was done they all had a stack of $7,000 each. All the extra bills, along with the fives and ones were Devon's. It had been his job, plus all of the evidence was up in his place. If anything went wrong, he would have the most explaining to do. They didn't have no choice about it anyway.

Keith couldn't wait to leave. Devon said, "Yo nigga, you got a date? get you a piece of this loot and take your ass on then."

He reached into the pile to get a piece of the jewelry that he wanted for himself. He picked out a ladies diamond engagement ring. Mike sorted through the watches and picked out a diamond studded Longines wrist watch. Naturally he put it on right then. Devon picked out a fat solid gold Gucci link chain with a chunky diamond studded pendant. Devon put everything back in the pillow case, and put it on his bathroom scale. "Alright ya'll, the bag weighs seven pounds. That's how much it's going to weigh next month when we take it to the pawn shop. He put the pillow case in his stash spot in his bedroom.

"So what's up with ya'll niggas? It ain't even lunchtime yet. I know ya'll ain't got shit to do, but you got to get the hell up out of here. Just don't make a bunch of noise on your way out. I've still got to live here, and I don't want to hear about that shit from nobody." That was the last time him and Keith put in any kind of work. He didn't know why, but Keith always acted like he was kind of nervous around him. Devon didn't really trust Keith that much anymore. Something just didn't seem right about him. It's like all he did was worry about what could go wrong. Nobody needs that kind of negative energy around them all the time. When you're doing something wrong, you want to believe in it. You need to think that it's going to turn out alright. After a while, negativity starts dragging you down.

Layla was on her way to the pawn shop to get her big bamboo earrings out for the second time in the past month. It was getting to be a routine she didn't like having on her schedule. Before she got all the way there, she watched a couple of guys go in ahead of her. They looked like they could have been on a mission, so she waited around outside until she knew they'd be into their business. Layla knew you could find out more about a nigga at a pawn shop window than you could from an hour long conversation. She waited outside for about ten minutes before she came through the door like one of the owners. Old Sammy Hiestel looked up from the two guys he was waiting on and nodded in her direction. She gave him her Angelina Jolie smile and walked around looking at the stuff hanging on the walls. She got as close as she could to the window though, she wanted to hear their conversation. "Listen man, it's a simple question, what are you ready to give me right now for all of it? One price for everything and it's yours. How long have you got to look at something before you know what it's worth?"

Sammy wasn't about to let himself get hustled. "If you want a price right now, for all of it without me checking it, all I can give you is $4500. That's the best I can do on short notice." The tall one said, "Man you must be smoking. This is seven pounds of damn near straight gold. Plus we've got watches and earrings with diamonds in here to go with it. If you can't come better than that we can take this deal to somebody who's serious about taking care of business. So what's your final answer going to be?" Sammy wasn't going to let these two push him into anything, and he let them know it, "Listen guys, when you leave with my money you'll be happy. After you leave I'm going to have to go over each piece of this used, and probably hot stuff to figure out how and where I can get it sold. I'll make a deal with you, I'll take all the gold off your hands for $3000. I'll let you keep the watches and precious stones for yourself." The shorter man said, "Come on Dee, we ain't got all day for this shit. If we get $5 G's for it all we can be out and move on." "You know this is not what we do, so let's just take what we can get and get gone."

Devon looked at Keith like he'd pissed on the floor, "Listen fool, we've done all the work and now this crack...." he stopped himself from saying cracker and went on. "This crack hustler wants to play us out of what we're supposed to get." Dee turned back to the window and said, "Alright, weigh up the straight gold and pay us for that. Everything else will be going to somebody who appreciates a bargain. I thought we could get a fair deal here, that's the only reason we came to you first. Now I don't know if we'll be back or not. If we do come back, this won't be the first place we try." Sammy thought it over and said, "Look fellows, I don't have that much money here right now. How about I keep the stuff and go over it tonight. Tomorrow I'll be able to give you what it's worth and I'll be sure how much I should pay. Everybody will get treated right and you'll know you can trust me to give you a fair deal." Devon thought about it for a minute and said, "If you don't play games with a man's money you can stay in business a long time. I'll be back when you open up tomorrow. Your final answer better be in cash. If it ain't the right number you don't have to worry about negotiating. Go ahead and weigh it all up right now. Make sure it still weighs that much tomorrow, and I want a receipt for what I'm leaving too."

Layla listened closely, and she knew these two handled the kind of business she was interested in. While Sammy was weighing up the jewelry Layla caught the shorter guy's eye. She crooked her finger and motioned to get him to come over there to her. He acted surprised that she wanted to talk to him, but he came over with a big smile. "Hello kitty, you got something to talk to me about?" Layla looked him right in his eyes and with a sexy smile said, "It's funny how you find things when you're looking for something else. I couldn't help but hear ya'll talking to old Sammy, if you want to get the most money for your stuff you should sell it one piece at a time. I know people that would love to see what you've got, I mean if you still own it that is." Keith looked over at Devon. "It's not all mine. My partner wants it turned into cash like yesterday." Layla said, "Maybe I should be talking to him too since ya'll are partners. Can you introduce me to your partner?" Without answering Keith looked where Devon was standing and said, "Yo Dee come over here for a minute." Devon's eyes shifted off Sammy for a second and looked over at Layla and Keith. He looked back at Sammy before he said. "Alright, come over here and check this out." He signaled with his head for Keith to watch Sammy weigh their loot. Keith stood by the window and Devon went to talk to Layla. "Good morning beautiful, my name's Dee and yours?" "My name's Layla Dee, and I hope it gets even nicer to meet you. I was just telling your partner there's other options for moving the property you've got. I have a lot of people I could show it to, and I'm sure I could sell it for you. The best way to get the most money is by selling it one piece at a time."

Devon could already smell what her angle was. She wanted to try and make a commission off each piece she sold. She was probably going to steal as much of it as she could in the process. "Well sugar, if I wanted to wait that long for my money we could do some business, but I'm only waiting until tomorrow. That's as long as I want to wait without seeing the reward for my work. I'd love to have more money, but time is worth more than money. I don't think we can do anything this time, but thanks for the offer. Why are you in here anyway? Maybe I can do something to help you out." When Layla looked at those two she told herself, "The only way they could help me would be as some body guards."

Instead of thinking out loud she said, "You know Dee, since you seem to know how to get your hands on valuable things, maybe we can help each other. It just so happens I know how to deal with valuable things. You know like credit cards and check books. If you ever run across any homeless wallets, they're sure to be welcome at my house." The way she smiled told Devon all he needed to know. She was an out of work paper hanger and wanted somebody to bring her the plastic and checks she needed to keep her working. It might be good having somebody like her on the team. Things could pay off even better if they had her skills around. "Ok Layla, maybe I'll get a chance to see what you can do sometime. How can I get in touch with you?" Layla pulled out her cell and said, "How about you giving me your number Dee, then I can have yours and you'll have mine." Devon told her his number and his jack went off with hers. "I'll be sure and call you if I come across anything interesting."

By now, Sammy was back at the window and Devon wasn't letting Keith take care of that business. "Excuse me Layla, I've got to handle things over there." He left her and rushed back to the window. Devon and Sammy picked up right where they'd left off. "Alright Sammy, I expect us to have a deal worked out tomorrow morning. You should really be adding in something for making me wait. You're keeping me from making a deal with somebody else today." Devon may have been smiling when he said it, but that didn't mean he wasn't serious. Keith went back to talk to Layla while Devon was at the window. "Looks like you and Devon had a whole lot to talk about. Have got something you need to talk to me about?"

Layla said to herself, "Ain't that cute? He wants to be in the loop. Well I can be sure to do that." "I think I'd rather talk to you Keith, your friend seems to be a little money hungry. That's alright if all you care about is getting money fast, but that's not the best way to go if you're trying to get the most. Let me have your number so I can call you and you can have mine." Keith gave her his number. "Well Layla, you know I might call you sometime so we can get a drink or something. Is that okay with you?" She smiled and made a kiss shape with her lips. "I'd love for you to do that when we're not too busy. Just don't forget to call me okay?" Keith looked at her shapely legs and said "How could I forget that? I can see you were put on earth to make men drool." Layla gave a shy laugh and said, "Thank you, but if you're drooling you probably need to grab a snack somewhere. You need to be hungry before you try to tackle me. I can guarantee I'm a whole meal baby." "That's good advice, I'll make sure to have an appetite the next time I see you." Devon was finished taking care of his business with Sammy, and signaled for Keith to come on. As they left, Keith held the door open to wave goodbye to Layla.

As soon as they were gone she went over to Sammy so she could get a look at what they brought in. When she saw how much stuff it was she said, "Wow, those two are a couple of busy beavers. I hope you let me get first crack at anything you want to get rid of. You know I'm always trying to increase my cash flow." Sammy looked up at Layla with his eyes slightly squinting and said, "Yeah they're busy alright, but they're probably in too much of a hurry. I don't think they'll last too long like that. If I decide to get it I'll make sure you see it first Layla. You know I'm always trying to take good care of you." For the first time, as long as she'd known him, she'd never felt a real nasty vibe from his old ass. But his time there was no mistaking it.

What had gotten into him to make him think that kind of move was going to work on her? Looking at him, she couldn't say that it was unexpected. Hell, maybe it could be to her advantage if she played her cards right. "Well Sammy, if you want to take care of me, why don't you let me hold my earrings today? I'm so broke it ain't funny, if you let me wear them for this job interview I'll never forget you for helping me put my best foot forward." Sammy didn't waste any time getting back to his normal routine. "If we were at my house maybe I could do something like that. But this is my business. I've got to make sure I take care of it so it can keep taking care of me." Layla almost smirked him but she held it in check. "Yeah Sammy that's exactly how I feel when I can't do something for somebody. But hey, that's the way life is. Just let me get the earrings out, I'll probably be back later to put them back in."

When Ellie got back from her vacation Tango told her it was time they brought Layla up to management level. There was too much going on with the club and whore house for her to handle it on her own all the time. If Layla started taking over some of the daily duties, that would take some of the pressure off her. Ellie had always been insecure about her position with Tango, and she didn't waste any time testing Layla. She had to know whether she was going to be a loyal bitch, or if she was just trying to get ahead by any means necessary. Ellie had never been so sure of her position that she didn't think the next bitch wasn't trying to knock her out of it. Ellie showed Layla the system they used, how to count the money into the book and then transfer the numbers over to the email system to come up with the daily total Tango kept.

Ever since Ellie started training Layla, she had kept back three hundred dollars from the total she gave Tango for his books. Every three months the program Jazmyn installed for Tango would give him a quarterly report. This time when he saw the report it showed his total was $3600 short. At first he was pissed at the idea somebody in there would steal from him, then he calmed down and decided he had to find out where the problem was. He was as calm as he could be when he came into the building that night. As soon as he got there he told Ellie, Layla and Freda to meet him in his office. When they were all sitting around the conference table Tango said, "I called you ladies up here because I'm confused about something. I'm hoping one of you can straighten it out for me. Is everything around here going alright? I mean is everybody satisfied with the job they're doing and how much money you're making?" All of their heads went up and down like bobble heads. Ellie was the first one to speak up. "Come on Tango what's the point of this? I've got to get back to my job before there's too much work to make up."

Tango didn't respond to what she said, he just sat there looking into each of their eyes one by one. "Ok the this is what this is about, I keep a running total of the money I take in over here. Every quarter I get a report that compares the entries to the books from what I take in from here. The problem this quarter is the numbers are way off from what they're supposed to be. They're $3600 off, and if I don't find out what the problem is I might have to start strip searching ya'll. This time it was Layla who was the first to say something. "I don't know how your money could be short Tango.

Every time I count it up, I write it in the book and then put it in the safe. If it's not coming up right then the books have got to be wrong. When you first put me in charge of this up here I've always kept my own copy of the books for the house. That way after I left the bar I'd be able to protect myself if anybody pulled a move on the money like that. We all know who they are so I'm going to wait until we hear the truth."

Ellie looked at everybody sitting around the table before she focused in on Layla. "I know you're not trying to say I took money from this man. I work too hard to have to steal." Layla wasn't about to back down from what she'd said. Her words were exactly what she felt was right. "I don't have to say you did anything, all I'm saying is I've got my own set of books. There's only one person that can get in the safe after I'm gone." Tango listened to them going back and forth before he said what really mattered. "Alright, now that we've got all of that out of the way, all of you need to listen to me. I'm not about to let something as important as my money missing go like that. There's too much money involved for me to pretend it didn't happen. Unless I find out what's going on I'm going to have to shut the whole place down. I bet somebody will come up for air to talk about it then."

Layla wasn't about to have her chance to shine be cut off without a fight. "But if you do something like that Tango, you'll be punishing the innocent right along with the guilty. I need the money I make in here to handle my business. Like I said, I keep my own set of books. I always make sure they're caught up with the counts from every night I closed. You can look at them and see how much money was there when I clocked out. That's got to be worth something to you." Tango put up both his hands as a sign of resignation. "See that's what happens when people don't care who gets caught up in their bullshit." Layla was hot about everything going on. She felt like she was the one on trial, it felt like all the attention was centered on her.

She really got hot when she noticed how calm Ellie's ass was. She didn't see how she could be sitting there like she didn't have anything to worry about, when she was the one responsible for everything that went down there. Why wasn't she concerned about how much money was missing? She should have at least been trying to defend herself or making up some excuse for not catching the thief herself. Freda was really the one caught in the crossfire, all she did was operate the bar. She had the most to lose if Tango shut the place down. Nobody's position was safe until Tango found out who took the missing money. Freda knew she could be replaced in a heartbeat so she tried to reason with Tango. "Tango, if you shut the whole building down you're going to lose more money than what somebody stole. I couldn't have taken anything if I turned in my bar money at the end of the night. It had to get counted along with all the other money right?"

Layla had to protect herself without making it impossible to work with Ellie. "Listen Tango, I need you to trust in me more than I need any money I could steal. If you check the books I keep against the records in your office, my numbers are going to match up with yours. That means anything that happened to the money happened after it was out of my control. I just want you to believe me and trust that I'm the same bitch I've always been." Ellie knew it was time for her to say what she'd been keeping to herself. "You know what Tango, I shouldn't even be sitting in here as a suspect. I've already proven how trustworthy and loyal I am to you." Tango wasn't about to let this little half slick bitch try to chastise him about how he took care of his business.

He glared at Ellie. "This ain't about nobody's personal references, it's about who's stealing from me and my business. When something is wrong you deal with it, and if you want to get it straight you check all the possible causes. I'm not going to let anybody take what's mine and pretend it didn't happen." There was nothing but silence and suspicious glances at the table after that. Then Ellie said, "Tango, I've got something I need to say about this. First, I'm glad your accounting system is working like it's supposed to be, and second I don't want you to question my loyalty or honesty without a good reason. The last thing I want you to know is I've got something here I've been keeping for you." She reached down in her purse and took out a fat stack of bills. She laid the money out on the table. "You can count it up if you want to, but there's the missing $3600 right there.

The fact is, I'm a better manager for you than anybody else in the world. I'd never let anything happen to hurt you if there's any way I could help it." Tango picked up the bundle of cash with a sour expression on his face. "I don't know why you thought you had to do something like this. If I didn't trust you I wouldn't have kept you in charge of so much of my business this long." Then Tango turned to everybody else. "I'm sorry you two had to go through this, but in a way I'm kind of glad it happened. Now you all know how much faith and trust I have in you. I'm depending on all of you to take care of my business just like you are now. I'm glad we all sat down together and got the problem straightened out." Layla wasn't ready to put the baby to bed just yet. Ellie had just put her in a very vulnerable position. The money didn't start missing until she took over the upstairs and got put in charge of the count.

"Tango, I need to know you still believe in me. Are you still sure about me and what I can do for you and your business? I know you're the truth because you picked me up and brushed my ass off when nobody else gave a damn. Thank you for believing in me then, but let me know if you still think I'm the one you want to handle your business." Tango could only smile as he shook his head and looked at Layla. "Layla baby, I wouldn't have let you get this close to me if I didn't already have a lot of trust and confidence in you. Just take a look around, all three of you are very important and valuable to me. Now let's all be happy we're still sitting here. I'm glad I didn't have to tell all of ya'll to get your shit and go home. If I didn't believe in you I wouldn't have asked any of you to tell me what was going on." Layla felt a little better after hearing that, but she wasn't too sure about Ellie's ass. Hiding the money and forcing the issue to that point made her nervous about what else she might be willing to try. Layla wasn't as convinced as Tango was about Ellie's loyalty. She resolved from then on to keep her eyes open whenever Ellie's ass was around.

After the meeting about the missing money was over Layla walked out thinking she had to make herself valuable if she wanted a secure future in Tango's operation. The whole thing had shown her just how shaky her future with him could be. She needed to get into a game of her own. One where she was in control of what happened and how the money got handled. She'd always been the type who wanted to know what side of the bed she was getting up from and how most of her money would get made. She was still pulling 12 hours in the house from hell with the bitches from Sesame Street. But now that her shift was over, all she wanted to do was get home and catch up on her 5 hours of sleep. She walked from under the awning looking for a cab. The beats from a maroon Cadillac STS in front of the building caught her off guard. She walked out to the street to try and flag down a cab. When she walked past, the car's electric window slid down. The sounds of Fantasia came out full force and instinctively she looked inside. It was the guy Keith she'd met at the pawn shop. With a big smile he said, "Hey there Layla, I've been out here waiting for you all night. Come on and ride with me so we can get a little breakfast. I want to talk to you about everything under the sun. That's about all we have time for since it took you forever to come out." Layla stopped at the window while peering in and said, "Keith right? You know you could have called to ask me if it was cool for you to drop by my business address."

Keith wasn't about to get put on a leash by her, at least not yet. "To tell you the truth, I hang out around here from time to time. But when I saw you coming out I wondered why I didn't already know you worked here. Now stop resisting and come on with me. I'll make sure we get what we both want. If it's breakfast I'll make sure it's good and hot. If there's something else you want maybe I'm still the man you need. I mean I am here with your ride ain't I?" Layla couldn't deny that he was there, and riding with him was definitely better than riding in a cab. His offer of getting breakfast was also the right thing to say. In spite of her fiercely independent streak, she accepted his offer and surrendered. "You have the advantage on me right now, so open this door so we can find out if our future can get started off on the right foot."

Keith smiled a welcome and threw the door open for his

sexy Amazon. He wanted to get next to her ever since they met at the pawn shop. Now she was nestled up next to him in his whip. Layla let herself sink into the plush leather seat, as she savored the aroma and texture of luxury. She'd always known her future was meant to be just like this. Her whole environment was going to be a reflection of where she led herself in life. She always said "led" when she talked about herself in the future. She didn't believe life was meant to just be lived. In her mind, everybody's life was an opportunity. It was given to everyone, and it was meant to be used to achieve big things. Whatever you did with that opportunity was up to you. It didn't matter where you were when you decided to seize it.

Layla snapped her head back upright when she became aware of her silence. She smiled sheepishly about taking the nap. "I'm really sorry Keith, I was sitting here with my mind lost in a whole other world. You also caught me being a little tired from work. Either that or you've got some kind of sleeping gas creeping up in here." Keith couldn't stop himself from liking the way she looked. Leaning back in the reclined seat, she was right where she was supposed to be. "Damn baby girl, you really looking fine right there. I could get used to having your fine ass beside me. A beauty like you is all I need to make my profile complete. You think you could get used to riding with a nigga like me?"

Layla smiled at his compliment, but she'd always been about making her own way. She wasn't about to hitch herself to somebody just because they were on their way to the top. She just smiled, she figured why not let Keith have his fantasy. "Baby, you should see me as a way to make things better, not just to look better. You can't just add me on like an accessory."

Keith drove and concentrated on her attractive features. While they were driving through the city they talked, until he pulled up at Pano's restaurant in Brooklyn for breakfast. When they parked he told Layla, "Come in here with me so I can feed you something to make you sleepy again. I know you like grits and eggs. They've got the best grits in town here." Layla's instant smile revealed that her hunger pains had defeated her stubborn nature. "You're going to have a hard time getting rid of me if you keep treating me like you know what you're dealing with." Keith liked hearing that. He made up his mind to do all he could to keep her around. "That won't be a problem if you're anything like what I think you are." He held the door open for her as they went inside for a booth.

Mike had been standing by the stairs in the hallway for more than a few minutes. He was waiting for Ellie to let him know when his load would be ready. It was Tuesday night and the work should have been finished. As soon as it was split into the two loads, him and Alphonso could pick up their shares and deliver it. After that they'd get their cut for the month and pick up the cash they were owed. For the last few months he'd noticed Monica and Devon hanging out with each other a lot more. There were even a few times they'd both been missing in action. Lately, the only time he caught up with her was when she was at the club doing hair. He wasn't feeling a lot of the stuff she was doing, like hanging around the bar acting like she was grown. He was going to tell her ass about it when he got the chance. She knew the bitches around there wasn't no role models for her.

As smart as she was, she really should have been in a school somewhere. She should have been spending time somewhere trying to get a skill. How did she think she was going to get ahead without any skills? She needed to get a square ass job and work that shit until something better came along. He wanted her to start building a future for herself. Mike laughed to himself when he thought about how he sounded. It was the same kind of shit Marlon used to tell him. For a split second he felt the sadness of regret because he hadn't listened to him. Ellie came down the stairs in a hurry and had to stop when she saw him blocking her path. Mike sensed the way her body instantly got tense. "Mike! What's going on? You waiting for me? I'm doing a million things at once around here and nothing's going like it's supposed to." The look on Mike's face showed he didn't give a shit. "Yeah, well I just want to know when the dope will be ready, I need to know when I can pick up my load."

She looked tired and worn down, but was too stubborn to admit the job was too much for her and beating her ass. "I can't give you a time until I know where it's at. I know it won't be ready until tomorrow." Mike shrugged and said, "Alright, just text me a time so I can pick it up. I've got some things going on and I need a schedule." She wanted to ask him what his business was, but thought better of it. She didn't have enough nerve for that, instead she said. "I'll let you know when they're ready. Just make sure you're ready alright?" "Yeah, thanks a lot." is all he said before heading for the bar.

When Mike walked into the back of the bar, Freda and Layla were having a deep conversation. It must have been a good one because neither one noticed him walking up. He sat down as close as he could to try and hear what it was about. He didn't really care, he was bored and wanted to get in their business. When they noticed him sitting there he played it off with a smile. "Hey there ladies, when can a man get some attention around here? Ya'll look like you're too busy taking care of your own business to give me any." Freda with a sly smile, tried to say something slick. "Well since this *is* where I work, if you any other kind of business you'll have to catch me when I'm not here. Since I'm always in here, I guess that means I haven't really got a life." Then Layla jumped in their conversation with both feet. "Looks to me like you're the busy one Mr. Mike. I see you come and I see you go, but you never stick around. If you're not staying around long enough to see anything, how are you going to know what's good? You've got to take your time to smell the roses."

Mike wondered why she was giving him so much conversation. "Why do you think I came over here? I wanted to find out what you two roses smelled like. The way the two of you were just going at it, I figured I might find out what I've been missing." Layla gave him a sly smile and said, "Hey, if it's meant for you, you'll get it. If you do what you're supposed to do nobody can stop you from getting what you want. So tell me Mike, are you doing what you know is right or are you too busy being a bad boy?" He took a few seconds before he answered. "I'm not saying I'm all that good, but you know what? Bad boys need love too. It takes a special woman to give their love to somebody when it ain't that easy you know?"

Layla's smile turned into a smirk. "It sounds like you're a lot of work to me. That sounds like the kind of job somebody with a whole lot of time on their hands would want. I know a girl that wouldn't mind taking the job but she's quite a bit of work herself." When she said that Mike followed her eyes up the stairs to where the hoes worked. Mike caught on and said, "You know what caliber of man I am, if you've got one that can fit my game bring her on. I make my decisions about women fast. It doesn't take me long to know if she's the answer for what I want." Layla turned up her lip before she said, "I've got one but she might be hard to let go of once you bite the apple." Mike smirked at that and said, "That's what I've been looking for, a woman I can't handle. When she's ready for me let her come. I'll take over from there."

Layla stood up and left Mike sitting at the bar. He stayed there, trying to wrap his mind around what he'd learned about his parents murder. His aunt being involved and the way the robbery happened, made him feel like strangling the truth out of her. But he knew he couldn't get anything straightened out until he knew everything. But one thing he was sure about was Ellie's ass had to go. He was going to let Tango have the satisfaction of taking care of her out. The only feeling he had in his heart for Ellie was hatred. The cold blooded anger he felt was what fueled his desire to see her time ended. It scared him to know that much evil was inside him. The world needed to be rid of her and everybody like her. How it happened didn't matter, as long as nobody else had to suffer. All the reasons she deserved it could get cleared up after she was gone.

As he contemplated the different ways he'd like to see her die he felt the gentle touch of finger tips on his shoulder. What he saw when he turned around blew all of those thoughts away. Death and revenge weren't on his mind anymore. It was that fine ass working girl Sheila from upstairs. She held out her hands, and like in a trance he stood up and took them in his. They embraced and began a slow sensual dance to Luther's "House is Not a Home. Mike towered above her slender frame but the tension of her body let him feel how strong she was. He felt the heat and response from her body. That made him feel like she was wound up as tight as a spring.

Mike held her gently but firmly in his arms and asked her what he wanted to know. "So tell me something beautiful, what made you want to come dance with me tonight?" She paused for a second with her head laying against his chest. "When I heard the music playing I felt like I was supposed to have a strong man in my arms." Mike smiled and said, "So is this my lucky day or am I just in the right place at the right time?" She laughed while snuggling even closer. "You're definitely in the right place at the right time, but whether you're lucky or not depends on what you know how to do." Mike could feel himself getting into the music with her. "I feel pretty lucky right now, so maybe I should take that chance with you." She pulled herself up on his chest and said, "You know what they say, nothing beats a failure but a try." Mike bent down until his lips were close to hers. She leaned her head back to let their mouths meet. They shared a passionate kiss and embrace right there on the bar's dance floor.

All Freda could do when she saw them was watch and smile. She had to shake her head too, she wasn't usually into snooping. But she had to admit that she watched them for a minute before she went back to washing the rest of the glasses in her sink. When the song was finished Mike and Sheila came over to the bar. Freda was standing there with a big grin on her face. "You two looked so romantic out there, you had me wondering if anybody would ever come and sweep me off my feet." Mike shook his head and told her, "Freda, you ain't nothing but an instigator. Is it alright with you if a man has a good time, sometime? I'll bet you've had plenty of chances to get swept up and only you know what you did with them."

Freda was still smiling when she said, "Okay, if that's what you want to think, but I'll plead the fifth. Now can I get ya'll anything before I shut all this down?"

Sheila looked at Mike as if it was up to him and he said, "You can let me have that bottle of Patron and after that you can have yourself a very good morning." She put the bottle on the bar and said, "That's the last thing I'm doing in here today, so you're on your own from now on." Sheila said with a smile, "You have yourself a good day Freda, we'll see you sooner than you want." After Freda left Sheila turned to Mike. "Layla said you were asking about me. There's a few things I'd like to find out about you too. If there's any questions about me you want to know, I'm the best one to ask. I'll tell you whatever I want you to know. Are there things you want to let me know about you?" Mike was the one who was smiling now. "Yeah well, there are some things I want you to know about me, but I think it's more important for you to find them out for your-self first. I want to know if you've you got a man somewhere that you'd call yours? But an even better question is, are there any men who consider you there's?" Sheila laughed and thought about it for a second. "I really can't help what some-body else thinks, but I know for sure, there's no man I've ever thought belonged to me. If a man wants to own me he's going to have to do a whole lot more than just think it or say it. Is that something you'd want to do Mike? Do you think you'd like to own me?"

Mike smiled at her and put up his hands and surrendered. "I think owning is something you do with property not people. See, I think all women are people, but sometimes they have to be treated like wild animals. See, I believe a woman is free, until she knows where she wants to be. When a woman really wants to be somewhere nothing and no one can make her leave." Sheila wrinkled her nose up and said, "So you believe in living and letting live? So how do you know if somebody is just for you? Don't you believe there's somebody for everybody?" Mike was waiting for her to say that. "When your somebody's just for you, don't you think they'll know it right away? Anyway, how do you know there ain't more than one somebody for everybody?" Sheila wasn't letting things go that far that fast. "We'll have to see how all that works out before anybody has any real answers."

Mike looked into her eyes and said, "Baby, I've been watching you around here for a little while. If you gave me a chance, you might find out you've been missing what's been right here all the time." Sheila cocked her head to the side like she didn't hear him right. "So you think I'm missing something?" She stood up, spun herself around in a slow circle. "Does it look like I've got anything missing to you?" Mike slowly shook his head as he watched her sexy tight body turn all the way around. When she stopped turning he just shook his head. "No baby, I think you've got all the pieces in the right places. The only thing you're missing is the right man to take care of it for you. The right man would love to take care of all that womanhood you've got." "Oh is that what you think? I guess I'll just wait for the right man to come along then. I've been looking for him, but that still hasn't paid off. When it comes to picking good men I don't trust myself. Maybe I'm the one that's getting lucky tonight. What do you think?" Mike was ready to agree but didn't want to sound too eager. "Only time will tell baby, but so far so good. Who really knows, maybe we're both getting started on a winning streak together."

Mike was still holding onto the note from Jazmyn and the contaminated straw Monica found. He was going to give it to Tango, but then he decided it would be better for him to wait until he knew for sure what Ellie's treacherous ass was up to. Mike didn't know whether he should just expose her or wait until she slipped up and got herself caught. Before he did anything he had to make sure Monica was protected. There was still a lot of information missing about what had happened to his parents. He wanted to wait until all of those loose ends were tied up before Monica got put into a bad situation. No matter what happened, the note from Jazmyn would connect the dots for Tango. He just had to be sure the accusations would stand up to all the questions Tango was definitely going to be asking.

Mike still took care of his business at the building, and when he did, he made sure to keep his eyes on Ellie. She jumped in and out of any of the whips at the house and move whenever she wanted. He would watch everything she did, but never caught her doing anything that would help him prove her guilt. He felt a little guilty because he was supposed to be a loyal worker, and doing this kind of shit made him feel more like a double agent. Ellie was the one who handled all the money from the dope game, so Tango would know right away if that wasn't right. As long as everything was good with that, nobody was going to question her about anything. He didn't feel too secure about what he was doing, and wondered if it wouldn't be smarter to just protect himself and take care of his sister. If he let things play themselves out the time would come when she'd have to tip her hand. Mike used go up to Tango's apartment sometime to talk about the operation, and Tango used to tell him to let him know how he thought things were going. Mike tried his best to let Tango know what wasn't being done right and what he should do to make it right, but Tango stayed a step ahead of him.

Mike told Tango him and Alphonso didn't like making the runs to the dope houses by themselves. He figured they needed to have some kind of protection or security on their cars. They had to be ready if anybody made a move on their load. They were vulnerable to be attacked when they moved dope around their turf. Tango said that would mean more cars and it would raise payroll. How was it worth it for some protection they didn't even know they needed? Tango thought Mike was just taking a healthy interest in the business, but started feeling kind of suspicious about all the questions. One day, he told Mike something he'd never thought about. "In business, everything shouldn't be shared. Sometimes, you have to take risks. You might have to follow your gut and believe in yourself." That meant was Mike was going to have to figure some things out for himself. The note and straw Monica had found was still eating away at him, and it had his baby sister on pins and needles. Mike didn't like watching her worry, but there wasn't much he could do about that. He wanted to confront Ellie and see what her story was going to be. Maybe that would make her see how much she had to lose. He'd tell by her reaction how true his suspicions were.

They took their deliveries out to the houses every two weeks. That meant they carried more dope between the 1st and 16th than they did from the 17th and 30th. Jazmyn had laid out the deliveries like that and Tango kept them that way. One night while Ellie was going over the books in the office, Mike asked her about it. "Say Ellie, how come we only bring the houses three keys on the 1st? They're always sold out before we come back on the 16ᵗʰ. I'd love to be serving the over flow after their dope from the first is gone." Ellie looked up at him like she was tired of telling people things. "Listen Mike, they can only sell as much as they have. If they had enough to sell all they wanted they'd have too much to get rid of if the police visited them. The only thing they'd be hustling up after that would be bail and lawyer fees.

You know there's a fine line between hustling sense and stupid greed. I hope you don't ever get those two confused." Mike thought about it for a minute. "Why can't we just move the dope out after the house shuts down? That way they'll only have enough inside to sell?" Ellie put down her pen and looked at him. "Because you'd moving dope through the streets twice. That's more trouble and more dangerous than it's worth. Just catching one case makes it too expensive to be worth it." Mike could see the logic, but he still wondered, "Why would a hungry bitch like her care about the risk him and Alphonso had to take? She wouldn't give a damn if one of them got popped making a delivery. All she was about was what was in it for her." While she was thinking about their dope schedule, he threw something at her from left field. "You know, I was thinking about the last time you came down to Florida. When you used to come, you never stayed with us. Did know anybody down there that you hang out with? Because you never used stay at the house with us. I remember you used to drop the dough off with my mom, and come back the next day to pick up the package. You didn't spend much time with us except the last time."

Ellie looked surprised that he brought up the last time they made the trip from Florida. But more than anything, she wanted to know why he'd brought it up. "You know Mike, I had been coming down there a lot before I started taking care of business with Marlon and Tanya. I'd been knowing the people I visited for a long time. Whenever I was in Florida, I didn't have any trouble hooking back up with them. They were some party people. You know Miami's got a reputation for throwing down with a party." Mike nodded his head in agreement. "Yeah, I know that's right. That partying is why a whole lot of niggas be losing their heads. That's why I always kept my head straight on my shoulders. You've got to always be ready for what might be coming next. If somebody wants to take what's yours, you've got to make sure they lost their head first." Ellie looked up at Mike trying to decipher his message, when she couldn't she gave up. "What just made you ask me about that out of nowhere? Is something going on I should know about?"

Mike put a smirk on his face he was sure Ellie couldn't miss. "It's just been on my mind a lot. You know, what went down when you got us up out of there, that's all. I've just been thinking about a lot of things." Ellie was even more puzzled then. "So what's there really left to think about now Mike? The past is gone and over with, we're all here now and all we can do is try to make sure the future is better." Mike didn't know what his next move should be. "You know Ellie, some stuff adds up and other stuff doesn't. I just want to get a lot of stuff straight in my head, you know?" Ellie didn't know what he was talking about but she knew she wasn't going to go there with him. Ellie mumbled, "Don't get hung up on anything that won't make your future better."

Mike acted like he hadn't even heard what she'd said. Then he said something to really get her attention. "You know what messes with me? You're my mom's sister right? I could never understand why we didn't go back for their funeral. Then I keep trying to figure out how them nigga's rolled up on my moms and Marlon like that. It was like they knew right where they was going to be. Like they was already waiting out there to rob them. You know what I mean?" By now Ellie's eyes had closed down into a couple of slits. "Are you trying to say something about me Mike? Because if you are you should go and have your head examined. I would never do anything against anybody in my family. I know you're not accusing me of doing some shit like that. If you know something say the shit with your chest. But if all you're doing is trying to start a bunch of shit up with me you've done it."

Mike knew he'd lit a fire under Ellie's ass, and he wasn't about to let it go out. He was going to have to let her marinate on that for now. His plan was to make his next move in Florida. Down there he could talk to some people who knew Ellie and what she was doing when she was there. Maybe they could tell him who she hung out with and what she was doing when she was down there. Maybe then he'd have a better idea of how to deal with what she's been up to. The next day, Mike went up to Tango's office. "Hey Tango, is it alright if I take a few days off? I want to make a quick trip down to Florida. Some people I know told me about some fly cars going up at an auction down there. I'll only be gone for a few days. I just wanted to see if I could take one of the cars out back?" "Come on Mike, you don't have to mess with no auction cars. I told you I was going to set you up with something fly. Give me a chance to get a few things together."

Mike didn't want to sound ungrateful, but he also didn't want to feel like he was being some kind of leech. "Yeah Tango, I know that, but you're always looking out for me. I just want to see what it feels like to do something for myself sometime. I probably won't even get anything. I just want to be on some grown man shit." Tango shook his head and said, "Alright young blood, go ahead and do it if that's what you've got to do. I know how it is, I was young one time too. Back then I didn't want anybody telling me how to do what I wanted to do." Mike didn't like lying to Tango but he really didn't have any choice. He didn't want to spill too much information before he had it all together himself. Before he hit the road he told Monica to make sure she stayed on the right side of Ellie. He'd be back in a few days and he didn't want her to set Ellie off until he got back. She was a little shaky about being there alone at first, but she understood what it was all about.

When Mike finally got back to Miami, he could hardly believe how much downtown Miami had changed. He couldn't believe he had to ask for directions to find places now. He'd only been gone 13 years, but now he hardly knew his way around. One thing that hadn't changed was where he had to go to get Monica some fresh gear. He headed for Lincoln Road, but he wasn't prepared to make his way through all those shops and stores. He envisioned having to get something from every one of them, but he still hated looking like a fucking tourist. The only good thing about it was all the hot Mamis out there licking their lips when he walked by.

It was frustrating trying to figure out what Monica was going to like. Mike went up to the finest one, out of the girls checking him out. "Hello beautiful, would you mind giving me a hand with something? My baby sister, back home, wants me to bring her a fresh wardrobe. I'm not ashamed to admit I don't know what that's gonna look like. Would you help me pick her out some nice outfits? I mean, if you did that you would really be helping me keep the peace. I'll hook you up with something cute too if you're in the mood to be nice to me." At first she looked like she wasn't trying to move, but when she heard she could get something, all of a sudden she got real energetic.

She twisted up her glistening lips and said, "I'll help you out since I'm really not doing too much right now. You're lucky you caught me while I'm resting between stores. When we're done, you're going to have to prove you appreciate me using up my time and fashion sense." Mike would have given her almost anything for taking this job off his hands. "Baby if you do this for me I'll make sure you're happier than I am about getting your help." She stood up with her hand on her hip trying to prove she had an attitude. Mike wasn't giving her his government. "My name's Meech and what do they call you?" Her nose wrinkled up when she laughed and asked him, "Meech? What did you have to do to get a name like that? I'm LeiArra but you can call me Lee Lee." "Okay Lee Lee, don't worry about how I got my name. Your mission is to get me a couple of bags of the freshest gear you can find out here. I've got a little hottie like you back at home, only she's my baby sister. Now get me the kind of gear you'd want me to get for a girl like you. She knows what she wants and what she's wearing has got to be fly. If you do that for me, I'll make sure you're happy you met me."

LeiArra smirked at him and said, "Nigga, all I need you to do is carry the money and follow me, I'll make sure you have all the freshest gear when you get back home. Plus your little sister will have all the extra accessories a sexy girl could ask for." After almost two hours and over $3,000, Mike and LeiArra's shopping trip was over. She looked disappointed it was over so soon. "Lee Lee, I want to thank you for all your help, I couldn't have done it without you. My sister's going to love the stuff you picked out. But I've still got some other business to take care of today. If I need some more of your help before I leave how can I get back up with you?" She smiled like she knew something he didn't and said, "Let me hold your phone." She took his phone and after putting in a few numbers he heard hers going off in the back pocket of her too tight shorts. "Put that number under fire extinguisher, if you need me or get in any kind of trouble don't wait. Just pull it out and use it okay baby?" Mike winked at her sexy smiling face before he walked away with the bags and all the dignity he still had left.

When he got back to the car, the only thing on his mind was a hot shower and a soft bed. He was feeling tired now. He'd driven around the city all day, so he decided to splurge on himself. He checked into the high end Blue Moon Hotel. He picked that one because when he lived there, he used to always dream about staying in it. It had been too high class and expensive for him back then, or maybe he was just too young and broke to get afford it. But either way, things were different now. This time he was going to take advantage. The only problem was he didn't have time to enjoy himself. He rushed through a shower in the luxurious bathroom and stretched out across the giant king sized bed. All he wanted to do was catch a nap. He knew he had to get rested before he started on the hardest part of his trip.

He didn't know what happened, but the next thing he knew he was waking up from a deep sleep. He checked the time and it was after 10 o clock. His mind was frantic, he didn't think he had enough time to find out what he wanted to know at the Pine Grill Tavern. His mama and Marlon spent most of their time there when they were hanging out. If they were working on a deal or meeting somebody about one, it usually went down in there. The way Oscar and Theresa ran the place, everybody treated it like it was their living room. They took pride in how they stayed hands on, but their eyes and ears were always open for what mattered around there. When Mike walked in he was shocked at how easily he recognized Theresa. What shocked him even more was when she flew from behind the bar and grabbed him. She tried her best to bear hug his breath out. She was the only one breathing hard when she let him go. "Damn boy, you done got big as hell! I ain't never thought I'd see you come strolling back up in here like this. Where the hell you been at anyhow?"

Mike just stood there smiling, remembering how much he'd always liked her. Back then, she'd always kept it a buck with him. Right now, he needed her to do that more than anything. "Tee I need you to tell me something." Theresa's answer was quick. "Baby, if you need to know something, all you've got to do is ask me." Mike took a minute to think about how he wanted to say what was on his mind. "You remember my mom's sister Ellie right? Theresa's face frowned up a little. "Oh, hell yeah I remember her crazy ass. She was always around here talking and acting like she was up to something real big. To hear her tell it, she was always in the middle of a major operation somewhere. Her ass stayed on her shoulders. She must have thought she was some kind of celebrity." Mike already knew that shit.

"Yeah well, I just want to know if you remember any of the

people she ran with? Do you know them or where they're at now? If you do, that would help me out a lot. I need to get in touch with anybody who'd know about what happened to my people. She said her friends moved around, but when she used to come down here she could hook back up with them people. Was she hanging out with any Jamaicans back then?" Theresa didn't say she didn't know what he was talking about, but the look on her face told him she didn't want to get involved in what he was talking about. With a serious look on her face she looked at Mike and said, "Listen sugar, some things are better left alone. I know nothing is better than the truth, but knowing too much can be the worst thing in the world. Your aunt was hooked up with some real shady characters." Mike wanted to know how much she knew about the people and where they were. "So Tee, if you wanted to put your hands on any of them could you? I mean, you know, just to ask them a few questions or something."

Theresa was careful with how much information she gave him. Her business depended on keeping things on the low. If she got known for spreading people's business, her spot wouldn't last long. "I can't say what kind of business she had with them, but she always wanted to do something big with them. She didn't want to mess with something if it wouldn't put her on top or close to it. They're still around, they ain't going nowhere. They've been running the same program for so long, all it's done is gotten stronger. They make it hard for all the other honest hustlers, they're Jamaican through and through. You know how it is with some folks, they're down for whatever pays the most the fastest. They get in on a lot of the robberies and kidnappings around here. If you look long enough, you'll see their mark on just about all of the dirt done around here some kind of way. The main thing I'm telling you to do is stay out of their way." He heard what she said, but his heart still pounded with a fury he wanted to unleash. Right then, all he could think about was taking his revenge.

His anger was too close to the surface. He had to calm down so he could think about what his next step would be. "So Tee, do you know where I can find these clowns? I promise I won't do anything crazy, I just want to know how I could touch them if I had to." Theresa didn't want to throw him in to swim with the sharks, but he had to know something that would give him some peace. "They've got a place in the Forest Shore Complex. It's one of those modern developments they built a few years ago. It's real upscale with security gates all around it. They've even got armed guards out there. My advice is you go back where you've been and stop thinking about those rodents. If you're thinking about doing something with them, you've got to make sure you're ready. They won't go down that easy, and you don't want to start something you can't finish." Mike already knew that, he was on a sightseeing tour this time. "Don't worry Tee, I won't do nothing stupid. I just want to find out what I don't know. When the time is right, it will be time to get mine. Thanks for being up on shit for me, you know I'll always love you baby girl."

Mike turned around and left the bar. But when he got back in the car he couldn't believe how bad his hands were shaking. He was so full of rage, he felt like he was swimming in it. He wanted to go exterminate those fools. If he finished them it wouldn't be anybody's loss. But he had to remember where he was. He didn't want to take his time this time. What did he have to sit down to think for? His mind was already moving too fast to have any good thoughts. That's the kind of kind of thinking that made mistakes happen. There's no way he could think anything through angry like that. Ellie had been down with them. Now that he knew where they were, what more could he do? It felt like his train of thought had run into a brick wall. He didn't have enough firepower with him to handle things right now. But at least now, he knew where to bring his version of justice. This time, he was going to have to leave without making a sound. He still wanted to hang Ellie's ass up so Tango could see her for what she was. He was going to let Tango handle her raggedy ass any kind of way he wanted to.

He drove back to the hotel and tried eating some room service food, but after a few bites all he did was pace the floor. He felt like the ball in a ping pong game. Every one of his thoughts sent his emotions flying between rage and strategy. He stayed around the hotel as long as he could, but around midnight he had to get out. He couldn't sit still, so he rode out to the Forest Shore Complex. Just so he could get a look around to see how things were set up out there. When he got to the place, it fit Theresa's description to a tee. It was sewed up tight with armed security guards and a concrete security fence all around it. There were woods on the backside away from the highway. It was some real rugged terrain, that would be hard to get through without your vehicles being seen. The rest of the area was lit up with bright lights and it was pretty well developed. What he had in mind wasn't going to be easy.

Mike just sat in his car, plotting and figuring out what his next move should be. He wanted to see the layout inside, but decided against going up to the gate acting like he was looking for a job. It was almost 1:30, he decided to try and catch Theresa at the bar. By the time he got back she was gone. Oscar was running things in there now. He could be a lot of help too if he wanted to be. He was just as good as Theresa was for knowing what was what and who was who. When Oscar saw Mike he started grinning from ear to ear. "Yo there young blood!" His mouth was so big he almost drowned out the DJ. Mike held up a hand and walked over to him. "The wind must be blowing downwind of a junkyard, because it's done blew some trash up in here!" Mike couldn't do anything but shake his head and laugh. "Yeah well, the wind must have been blowing this way a long time. Because they should have been missing this one nigga a long time ago." Oscar waved his hand at Mike and said, "Awwww nigga forget that noise, what can you do me for?"

Mike could see he wasn't feeling no pain, and since he was cracking himself up, it didn't make sense to try and stop him. "I thought your ass was over in Europe somewhere. What happened? Did they do something freaky and make you run your ass back here? I bet some of them French girls tried to ménage a trois your ass. You've got to always have some back up with you when you run up on these hoes. Next time you run up on one of them French hoes you'll know better." Oscar always kept some shit going, but Mike just smirked at his ribbing and waved him off. "Ain't no French or no other type of freak can run me nowhere. Ask any of these bitches about me. They'll all tell you I'm him. When I hit it I wrecks it, and it don't go the other way around." Oscar shook his head before he said, "Yo my man, cut the bullshit, what's been doing you right out here?"

Mike sat down at the bar and rested his elbows on the rail. "Man, the only thing treating me right is my left hand and I think it's been cheating on me too." Oscar laughed as he made his way over to Mike. "Yo Oscar, I know your ears be in on some of everything going on around here. What can you tell me about these Jamaicans that be putting in all the work around here?" Oscar looked down the bar and leaned in closer. "Why you trying to get me caught up in their bullshit? You know I mind my own and let the Devil do his own work." Mike wasn't trying to waste time, he figured it was best to just tell him what he wanted to find out. "Man, I need some info on the Jamaicans that stay out in that Forest Shore Complex. What can you tell me I don't already know?" Oscar looked long and hard at him when he spoke. There wasn't any laughter in his tone. In a low and serious tone he said, "Listen to me, those niggas ain't about nothing but trouble.

Whatever deal you got going on with them needs to get handled another way. I don't want you stretching yourself out around where them niggas stay. They stay ready to do dirt, and they don't mind putting a nigga up under some of it either. Make sure you got the upper hand when you do come their way." Oscar meant well, but Mike was impatient and frustrated. He was feeling all the pressure of a bomb with a slow burning fuse. "I hear you big O, I'm not doing anything until I know it's going to go down the right way. I just want to see if you know how I could get next to them. If I had some names of somebody they trust, I could get plugged in with them." Oscar could tell Mike wasn't going to let it go. Oscar slowly shook his head."Alright, listen to me hard head. The best way you can probably hook up with them is by their connections down in the Sweatlands. They got corner workers down there hustling crack all day. As long as they can get a blast, they'll stay out there all night. Just roll down there and tell one you want some weight. They get all their dope from the Jamaicans, they'll hit you with whatever you want.

I'm telling you boy, don't go messing with them fools unless you plan on leaving them cold."

Mike looked at the man's worried face and told him, "Thanks Oscar, you don't have to worry about me, I'm just sniffing around right now. When I'm ready to start cleaning things up, I'll be bringing all the right equipment with me, trust me." When Mike left, he headed over to Liberty City. That's where the Sweatlands were, as Oscar called it. A fresh ass STS sporting New York plates was sure to catch their attention. After making a few passes through the block he pulled up next to one of the lookouts on the corner, "Yo what you got for $50?" The kid nodded his head and the biggest dude in the crowd ran over to the car. He reached out his hand in the window to show him a rock the size of a walnut. "This here is a fifty, but I can let you get one of these six's for $75. If you want to fly right I can keep you going all night!"

Mike looked coldly into his eyes and said, "Nigga do I look like I'm trying to get high? Give me this fifty, and if it's right I'll be back. When I get back I'm going to want to know what you can show me for some weight. How long is it going to take you to get your hands on a bird?" With a puzzled look on his face the guy said, "I don't know right now but here go my number. He handed Mike a card with a cell number on it as he took the 50 out of his hand. Call me when you're ready to move and we'll get it together for you." Mike went back to his room and waited about an hour before he dialed the number on the card. "Ya mon, wat you want mon?" Mike heard the heavy Jamaican accent and said, "I want to see if you can get me a bird man. What's up with that?" The guy was quiet at first like he was waiting for directions. "It's gwana be 35 time an it's gat ta go don when ah say." Mike said, "I got to check mine and I know you want to check yours, so how's it going to happen?" The Jamaican guy said "When ya ready ya call me back. When ah know ya mean business we a get all a dat together real soon." Click. That was all he needed to know, it was time to move.

He went back to the hotel, and tried to sleep. He had to be ready for that ride back to New York. As soon as he woke up, he hit McDonald's, grabbed a sausage biscuit, and hit the road. Mike made it back to the city in a little under 12 hours. He'd pushing the Caddie like it was meant to be pushed, and she responded like a stallion every step of the way. Every time he pushed the pedal she let him know there was still room for more. When he got back to the building he was as tired as a runaway slave. When he fell through the door and saw Monica, he said, "Yo baby girl, where's Dee at?" She was so surprised and happy to see him, all she did was jump up and down, pulling on his arms asking him to tell her what he had for her. She hadn't even heard what he said to her, all she wanted to know was, "What'd you bring me back big bro? I know you got me something good! Come on where's my bag at?"

Mike was so blurry eyed and weak he could hardly stand up. The way she was pulling on him and asking him what he had for her, he was ready to fall in the floor. When he couldn't take any more he said, "Come on lil nigga. if you don't quit pulling on me, you're gonna make me fall out in the floor, then you won't gonna be getting nothing. "That's the only reason she stopped long enough to see how he was wavering on his feet. He still felt like a drunk when he asked her again, "Come on, where's Dee at?" Now she was really mad. "How you sound looking for Devon's ass? When you know I ain't trying to think about him before I get the stuff you got for me? Are you thinking straight?" Her stiff crossed arms let him know what kind of attitude she had. "He's so busy running around here with that Keith nigga don't nobody know where his ass at. He's probably in the same bags my stuff is in, where is that at?" He laughed at the way her face was all frowned up. "You is one spoiled ass little brat. Don't you know that?" With her head cocked to the side smiling she said, "Yeah I been knew that, but I don't know what you brought me back."

He finally gave her the keys to the car. "Go look in the trunk and take out whatever you can carry, just don't mess with my suitcase." She was gone before he could finish talking. With her busy ass out of the way he made it to his room and fell across his bed. Before his shoes were all the all the way off he was snoring. Monica came back in so fast it seemed like she'd only been gone a few seconds. He woke up to her high pitched screaming, "Ohhhh weeeee, I love you Mikey, you're the best. You got me out all the freshest gear. This here is all the best stuff. Everything is straight hot to death. These nigga's tongues will be hanging out they mouth when I roll out in this hook up." When she said that his eye lids fluttered open. "What did you say? I know you don't think you about to be running around here acting like you no little hoe!" She stopped twirling around in the spot on the floor. With all of her attitude she said, "Hold that up right there bro, you can miss me with that. I know you don't think I'm the one or the two. Ain't nooooo nigga can come up and say I gave him none of this." Slapping her butt for a sound effect. "You better take it back before I have to slap your face." He was too tired to end up trying to fight her little wild ass. "Alright baby girl. I just have to check your ass sometime. I'm the only one you've got to make sure you stay real in the game. You know how much I love your crazy ass, just make sure you don't forget it." She collected her loot and ran over to her room as he passed back out.

All Sheila could think about after they shared their special dance that night was Mike Hall. Her mind was feeling all cluttered and cloudy, but how was that possible when he was the only thing on it? She kept thinking about what was up with him, and where was their relationship going to go. Thinking things like, "Things are really going good with this new man. The way he was doing his thing was definitely what she was waiting to see." These were new thoughts for her. The way they swirled around in her head made her feel good all the time. She wasn't the head over heels falling in love type, but this guy had thrown her whole game off. She was seeing him in a new kind of way, and thinking about him all the damn time too. Sometimes she thought he was too cold and distant, but even that was alright with her. He probably had been hurt by a woman before, or been disappointed by one. Now that he had his shield up, she would have to be the one to break it back down. He wasn't going to make it easy for another woman to make him a target. Sheila Garrett wasn't the type to be sitting around thinking about any man unless she could see something in the deal for her. All Mike could offer her was a piece of his future with him. That wasn't really such a bad thing was it? She didn't even know if she was ready for that yet. Unexpectedly a warm hand closed around hers.

She didn't say anything, she turned around and saw Mike's grinning face. He'd been standing there staring at her the whole time. "What were you thinking about sexy? Whatever was on your mind must have been deep. I couldn't have gotten up on you like that if it wasn't. I'll bet it was something sexual or was it some real freaky shit? That's about the only thing that could have your mind tied up like that." Her face burned from blushing. It felt like he was laughing at her, and the thought made her mad. But she'd still forgive him if he kissed her. She didn't want to let him into her heart so easily, but it was already too late for that. She gave him something to think about. "Some of us little people have financial issues sometime, so we've got to get our mind right to handle our business. I have to concentrate if I want to make some of those money problems go away. That's how I come up with the plans and schemes I have that bring in cash. These days I'm making something out of almost nothing." Now she laughed at him because of the face he was making. He smirked and said, "Did you forget? You're supposed to be Superwoman, remember? You're the one who's always playing all that Miss independent, I'm a boss, and all that extra shit. Should I go on?" Sheila just gave him her dirtiest look. "I hope you know, nobody likes a smart ass. I was wondering if I should tell you something that could get the both on the right track. I'll know when you show me you want to make things better for me and you."

She had Mike curious now. What kind of secret was she keeping from him. Why would she say something like that? If it was something she didn't want him to know about, why would she start talking about it? "You haven't been holding out on me have you? I wanted to believe you were being true to the heart with me, but you've got me thinking I need to switch up." Sheila didn't want to lose any ground she already had. "Oh no baby, believe me, I'm going to always hold that space with you. I just don't know if you want to stay there with me. We've got to be that way with each other. If we don't, how far do you think we can go?" All Mike could think was,

"She is turning herself into a real puzzle, maybe she was the one, out of all of them, he couldn't figure out." In a serious tone of voice he let her know what was up. "I can't let you know how I feel about something unless you tell me what you're talking about." Sheila looked into his eyes and decided to trust what she'd been feeling in her heart.

"Mike, we could get our hands on a lot of money, and we won't have to worry about police coming after us or any investigations either. As long as we keep quiet, nobody will know what happened. If you're down I'll tell you everything. I just need to know you're going to treat me right after we get the money." He was excited about the idea of getting a lot of money. But that's all it was, an idea. He needed to know the details before he could decide if he was going to be down or not. "Baby, when we come up I'll be more than right to you. I'll be the best man you've ever seen. Ask yourself, haven't I already been treating you right? I'm still going to be that way when everything is done. Sheila was smiling because she already knew he wasn't going to do her wrong. She just needed to hear him say it. "I know things are gonna work out once we know where we're headed together. I know somebody that's been making payoffs every other month to the police. There's a briefcase full of money in the trunk of his car when he meets them at the Queens Place mall. They're up there waiting for him on the top floor of the parking garage to take it out." Mike knew what kind of job this was going to be, and he couldn't wait to get his plan together so he could knock it off. "Damn baby girl, that's a sweet lick for us. Get me all the details and tell me how to identify the driver. After that, we will be straight paid." The only answer he needed was the smile she gave him when she went back up the stairs.

Whenever Devon wanted some time alone or just felt like being quiet he would go up on the roof of the building where nobody could bother him. It was times like these when his thoughts would come and fill up the quiet spaces in his head. He'd have thoughts about his mom being gone, and how he didn't have anybody close to him anymore. These kinds of thoughts made him feel alone. Keith was supposed to be his boy, but that was way back when. Now all that nigga did was run the street with crackheads and hypes. He was always on a mission, trying to make a dollar out of fifteen cents. Whenever he saw Money now, he had a bag of dope in his hand or he had one close by. Everybody knew Monica's brother Mike was nothing but a loose cannon. Riding around in that big black Escalade looking for an excuse to go off. Most of the time he was alright, but everybody knew his setting was just a couple of clicks away from berserk. Monica's crazy ass was all over the place too. Most of the time she was cool, but there wasn't nothing you could do with somebody who acted like a little girl. It was easy to forget how young she was because her body looked like it belonged on a grown woman. She looked good and was ready to get smashed. You couldn't blame a grown man for trying to get some.

Tango was busy being the boss of the whole world. But he still had time to keep everything going smooth around there. Nobody wanted to see what it would be like if he let his crazy side go. He had all the respect of the people who knew him. He wasn't ever going to lose that. For all of his power over everything, it still seemed like whenever Devon was around he got sad. Maybe Devon made him think about Jazmyn. Tango was never going to accept how she died, it was too sudden. Then for it to be a drug overdose, by somebody who never used any kind of drugs? That only made it even harder to take. He couldn't help but feel responsible for it because he hadn't protected her. The worst part was, whoever was actually responsible for it had gotten away with it. Who could have caused her death from an overdose? That question had to be eating his soul up. He still hadn't dealt with it, and everybody around him knew that it was unfinished business. He blamed himself for being too busy taking care of everything and everybody except her.

Devon took his mind off what happened to his mother by pulling stick ups. Him and Snake were looking into hitting some of the big churches, but Monica's nosey ass heard them talking about it. She was a fucking trip. She hadn't snitched on them yet, but you never knew if she would either. Devon tried to stay cool with her, but he knew she was crazy. When he looked at her now he couldn't help but see how fine she'd gotten. She'd been like one of the boys or a little sister before, but now shit was looking way different. It was like she grew up overnight. One day when they were out on the stoop he asked her, "Yo Moni, who you giving that pussy to? I know your ass got a couple of boyfriends or at least a couple of booty call ass niggas." At first she didn't say anything. She blushed and looked at her feet. Then she said, "You don't have to worry about what ain't none of your damn business. I'm the only one who needs to know who I'm getting this pussy to. But I'll be sure I let you know all about it right after I give it to him." Devon cut his eyes at her and in a teasing tone said, "Oh, now you've got some secrets huh? Whatever you do in the dark is going to come to the light." He gave her a suspicious look and teasingly shoved her shoulder. He couldn't believe she was still blushing. "Whatever I decide to do ain't got to be in no dark. Anyway, you don't need to worry about what I'm doing. You'd better be making sure you don't get your dumb ass caught up out here. He just smirked her and said, "Ain't no shame in my game baby. You ain't got to be all up in mine. If you want to know something about a nigga like me all you've got to do is ask around."

No matter the time that went by, Devon was still walking around in a daze. He couldn't get his mind right after his mother died. Him and Monica were as close as they'd ever been, but when he felt lonely, and she was there, he wanted to do things with her. He didn't want anybody to know about that part of him. That kind of stuff made him go up to the roof. Devon sat up there to let his mind rest. It was the one place he had where he could get away from everything. There was an old set of car seats up there Alphonso had taken out of one of the cargo vans. Sometimes he'd stay up there for hours, watching the clouds go by. He'd talk to himself about things he didn't want to talk to anybody else about. Up there, his imagination could take him places where his mind was safe. Where he didn't have to deal with what was real for a while. He remembered growing up in Virginia, and how they had trees and grass growing everywhere. He missed going off in the woods by himself. He laughed thinking about the racist white kids at school. How they used to try and hurt him on the sly. What was funny, he already knew what they were up to so he made sure to hurt them first.

Lost in his daydream, suddenly Devon felt something crawling on his neck. He tried to jump up quick before it went down his back, but that made the car seats flip over. The seats turned over and fell on top of him. All he could hear after that was laughter. He looked out from under the seats and Monica was doubled over laughing. "Monica!" She was laughing so hard she was out of breath. She had tears in her eyes and could hardly talk. When she caught her breath she said, "Oh snaps Dee, that was fucked up. I thought your ass was supposed to always be on point!" He was hot at her ass, so he barked on her hard. "Man that shit ain't funny, Your ass ain't even got no business up here. What is you creeping up here for anyway? Probably spying on me or some other type of bullshit." She wasn't taking that from him, and let him know it. She straightened up from laughing at the spectacle he'd made of himself. "Nigga please, your busted ass should be flattered if I'm paying attention to you. I can go anywhere I want around here, you don't own shit. So what?"

He knew it didn't make sense to argue with her crazy ass, so he turned the volume down. He needed to do that to bring her ass back to earth. He was still shaking his head when he set the seats back upright and sat down. "Alright alright, pump your damn brakes. Why do you have to always take shit to the extreme? I don't care what you say, you ain't got no business up here messing with me. I'm minding my business, and here your ass come playing stupid ass games!" She could see he didn't want to fight so she decided to give him his space. "If that's how you want to be, stay your ass up here with your damn self. I thought we was cool and shit. I ain't know you was on some old weak ass shit like that. I'll leave you alone so you can finish jerking off in peace."

She turned around fast so he couldn't see her laughing. That just pissed him off again. "Your little dumb ass don't know what I'm up here for. You square as a pair of dice, talking about I'm jerking off. I don't have to jerk off, I got bitches to do that shit for me. Anyway, your virgin ass don't know nothing about jerking off. If you do, it's probably because you been on line checking out porno or something. I know your tight ass ain't fucking nobody. It's too many niggas walking around here with their dicks in their hands. They're all waiting to see who's got the winning ticket to hit that jackpot." He was cracking himself up, but she wasn't laughing. "Ha ha ha nigga. I don't know what you laughing for, you just like the rest of these dumb ass niggas. Ain't none of ya'll got a chance. You're all so stupid, you wouldn't even know how to read the ticket. If you had the right numbers you'd be too dumb to cash it in."

When Devon saw the way her face changed he stopped laughing. Now that she was her mad at him he wanted to make peace. "Come on Moni, I don't want to have to fight with you. Why you always fucking with me though? It's like pushing my buttons gets your ass off. What did I ever do to you?" Monica didn't say a word, she just sat down next to him with her chin in her hands. She looked as miserable as he'd been looking a few minutes earlier. She slumped her shoulders and said, "I just want to know how come you ain't never nice to *me*? I be watching how you talk to everybody else, you be all nice to them. You laugh and talk to them all the time like everything's alright, but when it comes to me it's like you've always got a attitude or something. Like I'm the one that pissed you off. How come you're always in a bad mood with me?"

Devon felt wrong for making her feel bad. He didn't want that on his conscience, so he put his arm around her to pull her closer to him. He wanted to make her understand how things had to be with them. "Come on Moni, you don't understand how it is with us. You're a big girl now, and you're fine as fuck. When we were kids and shit it was cool. You know, we used to run around and hang out together. But that was a long ass time ago. That's how it was supposed to be, we were just kids. Now we're both too old to just be being cool like that. I mean, I still like you and everything, but you're too beautiful to be hanging around me now. It's really not smart for you to be close like that with me no more.

Sometimes when I see you around here, I be wanting to put my hands on your body. We've been down too long to be getting on some shit like that. I mean, that's damn near like some kind of incest or some shit. I just be trying to stay away from you and making sure you keep a safe distance from me. If I didn't, I could see me doing things to you." Monica still had her head down, and wouldn't even look up when she said, "Thanks a lot for looking out for me Devon. You know, I'm still just a little girl. I've got a woman's body but I don't know shit, right?" Then she looked in his eyes and said, "My little girl mind ain't got no idea what I want to do huh?. You and Mike are probably right about me. I'm so stupid I'd probably go fuck a lot of guys just to see what it feels like. It's a good thing I got you and him around to keep me from having a fucking life. I'm so lucky"

He couldn't believe the shit she was saying. He pushed her back so he could get a better look at her face. But when he did, all he saw were tears. He was shook when he saw that she was crying. He felt helpless and didn't know what to do. "Moni, what's the matter? I mean, what are you crying for? Don't you know that means I care about you? I don't want to be one of them niggas that hurts you or breaks your heart. I don't want you to end up hating my ass. You already know how much you mean to me. How do you think it's going to look if we start being together like that? Your crazy ass brother would straight bug out if he thought I was fucking you. That nigga would try to skin my ass piece by piece. I'd have to get away from around here or kill his crazy ass." She almost burst out laughing from the look on his face. "Dee, you is so stupid, he already think we done did it. He knows I'm damn near grown, and ain't nobody getting none of this unless I want them to."

She stopped talking and pushed her face into his. When their lips met they kissed and let their emotions take over. At first their kiss was timid and curious, but soon it became urgent and passionate. They didn't try to put their tongues down each other's throat, but they liked how it was feeling. Slow and curious at first, it grew in intensity. When they stopped and looked into each other's face, they knew they didn't want to stop anymore. Monica leaned back and Devon looked almost as calm as when she'd watched him sleeping. With his eyes still closed he pulled her close to kiss her again. This time they kissed with passion and a hunger for the love they were both feeling. That night they discovered the power of love, and the feeling they'd been keeping buried inside was out now.

It seemed like Monica was always worried about Devon. She couldn't help it. She always wanted to know where he was and what he was doing. It was like they had some kind of connection that she couldn't stand to be broken. If she knew he was down the hall by himself, she made up some excuse to go down there. That morning she woke up too early, and when she tried and couldn't go back to sleep, instead of turning on the television, she got out of bed went down the hall. She knocked on his door and he answered it half asleep, "Who is it." "Hey Dee, want some company?" Devon just opened the door and rolled his eyes. "It don't make no differ-ence to your ass if I want company or not, you still ain't going nowhere." She laughed and pushed him out of the way. "Quit fronting, you know your ass don't want to be by yourself. Without me you'd be lost and turned out." He shook his head and walked away. "Tell yourself anything you want, but you better believe I'm going to be alright. You're the one that needs a damn hobby. I just don't know if Mike or Ellie will let your ass have one."

When he started laughing she let him have it, "Yeah nigga whatever, I bet you when I get on my own, ain't nobody going to tell me nothing. I'm gonna to do whatever I want, and don't you forget it. All my brother be doing is looking out for me. You need somebody to look out for your dumb ass." He wasn't letting her turn that shit back on him. He told her how it was in his world. "I don't need nobody to do nothing for me. When I've got enough money together, everybody can just stay out of my face." She'd run out of words to argue with him a long time ago. She stood in the middle of the living room with her hands on her hips, shaking her head and smirking. "Dee, you're going to have to get yourself together sooner or later. If you think don't nobody around here know what you're doing you're crazy.

Tango wants you to stop sticking everybody up and come work for him." As soon as she said Tango's name he knew he had to stop talking to her. There was no way she was going to let it go. When she said that, he put his hands up. "Come on, you know Tango wants everybody in the world to work for him. If he had his way he'd stop hustling and be king of the world. All I want to do is get away from around here. If you can't stop coming down here running off at your fast ass mouth, I'll be getting out even faster." Monica just stuck out her lips and said, "Nigga, I'm the only reason your ass is still hanging around. If you woke up and found out I was gone you'd lose your damn mind." He tried to mean mug her but couldn't. She knew he was fronting when he started smiling. They both ended up laughing and watching cartoons. Still in denial.

Devon knew it was time for him to get away from Tango's building a long time ago. Too many people were watching him and watching it. It was time for him to have a place of his own. If he was ever going to make his own way in the world, it had to be out from under everybody's nose. Being so close to Tango and Ellie was a drag on his lifestyle. The more he thought about it, the more he had to admit he really just wanted to be with Monica. That was a scary thing to admit to himself, but he had to face what he felt inside. They were together most of the time anyway. It just felt like there was always somebody watching what they were doing. One day Devon was riding down Harvard street a for rent sign in the window of an old looking brownstone caught his eye. It was right on the corner of 178th street and Harvard. It looked in good shape and was pretty clean. It had a nice front stoop with some flowers in a planter on the outside. It was just the kind of nice quiet little place he was looking for. He could fall back there whenever he wanted to get missing. It also had an alley running behind it.

When he rode by and went down the street he couldn't help thinking how cool it would be to have a back way to come in and out. He put the number from the sign in his phone and told himself to call it when he got home. It felt right because it wasn't too far from the building on Mercer.

When he wanted to get away from over there, he would have somewhere close by he could go to that was quick and easy. When he got back and saw Monica he asked her about it. "Big head, do you want to get somewhere out of here to live? You can be down with me or you could keep on waiting for your brother and aunt to tell you what to do. What do you want?" Monica's lip curled up when she said, "Nigga I can already think for myself. If I ever do need something from somebody, I know who I could ask for it. How are you moving somewhere on your own when you ain't even got a job? You probably can't even take care of no place by yourself. Who's going to cook and clean up behind your sloppy ass? I know you don't think I'm trying to be no maid for your ass."

She looked at him like she needed to hear him say the words women swear makes all the difference. "Awwww come on, now you tripping. Why would I need you for that? I don't need no maid or no cook either. I already know how to clean up behind myself, and if I get hungry I know how to find me something to eat. I eat out all the time anyway. I'm just letting you know I want you to be with me when I wake up and go to sleep. You know, you do be keeping me from doing bullshit sometimes. I just want to know I've got you in my corner all the time." He still hadn't said the words she wanted to hear, so her mind still wasn't made up. She wanted to see if he was serious about becoming a grown man. "When I can see that you're ready to be real I'll be in your corner, but if you keep trying the same games you've been running with me, I'll be gone. It's up to you what I do, but you'd better be sure about how serious you are. How much are you willing to change to make me happy?"

Devon was already sure he wanted her to be with him

when he left. "Moni, you know you're what I need to be happy, and you already know nobody's perfect. If you work with me, I'll put up with you and all your spoiled bullshit." He smiled so she'd know he was kidding, at least a little bit anyway. She leaned up in his face before she said, "If you don't know the three little words you need to get me in your corner I guess you don't know enough to have a woman like me." Devon took her by the shoulders and pulled her close until their lips were close. He breathed out slow with his lips against hers. "Moni baby, you know I love you, I can't stop wanting you and don't want to see you with anybody else. Telling you that shit over and over ain't what makes it true. I want to know if you're ready to do what I want you to do. Are you ready to come be with me? I promise I'll prove everyday how much love I have in my heart for you. We can do together what neither one of us can do by ourselves." Monica nestled her head against his neck and whispered, "Show me what you mean and I'll believe it when I see it."

Devon called the number for the apartment. When he talked to Mrs. Ellis he knew the apartment was where him and Monica would be. The lady was a whole trip, and talked a lot of junk, but still kept everything about business. She told him she wanted somebody in there that was about their business. It was a good deal because she was only charging them $1500 a month for a two bedroom upstairs apartment with utilities. They didn't have to pay a security deposit as long as they moved in right away. She said she was tired of the thieves and criminals around there casing her place out. She didn't know if they were plotting a burglary or an arson, but she lived by herself, and it was no telling when one of them might try their luck.

Devon said he'd start moving in the next day. He promised her nobody was going to bother her or her property as long as she knew him. As soon as he got in his car he called Monica. "Hey baby, I might need you to help me get some stuff in my new place." He could almost feel her smiling through the phone. "New place? What are you talking about?" "I just rented us an apartment. You need to give me a hand with some of this stuff." He was excited and she was as happy as him. "Okay baby, I'll be over there to help you as soon as I'm finished with these heads. If you really need me you can come pick me up now." He wanted to get her, but he didn't want to look too desperate. "I would come and get you but I've got to finish packing this stuff up. Call me when you're finished and I'll come get you. I mean, I'll come and get you like you want to be got."

It didn't take long to get moved in since they didn't really have any furniture. All they had was what was at Devon's apartment. He left most of that stuff in there. By the time they got finished unpacking and moving their stuff to where they wanted it, they were both tired and sore. The feeling of independence was better than either one of them thought it would be. No one could know how much they needed freedom and peace until they lost them. It's exactly the same when you have them for the first time. If you've never known what it was like to be free, it felt like you were getting let out of a cage. Time and their problems seemed to fly by. Nobody around there could figure out what happened to Monica and Devon. They didn't tell anybody where they were living, so they were all left wondering what was going on. They still came by the building through the day, and even slept there some nights. Monica only told Mike where she was staying. She had to let him know right away where they were. She had to let him know what was going on. She wanted to make sure he was cool with them being on their own. She figured she owed him that much. Devon wished he had somebody he could talk to about things, but he was glad he at least had Monica. Devon told Tango where he moved to so he could get to him if he ever needed to. Devon told Tango he got the place so he could feel like he was on his own. He couldn't grow if he didn't have a space of his own to do it in.

Tango took everything he said real smooth. He even told Devon if he ever needed him for anything to let him know. Tango let Devon keep the keys to Jazmyn's old place. That way he'd always have somewhere in the building he could come to. Ellie on the other hand, had a whole lot of extra noise she wanted to say to Monica. She started the whole thing off by telling Monica she was acting like a hoe. Talking about her coming there in the morning and staying out all night wasn't what a decent young girl should have been doing. That made it seem like she was staying out more than she was staying in. Monica told her she was only hanging out with her friends and was alright. Monica was still coming down to the club though. She kept doing the girl's hair for extra money and even helped out behind the bar some nights. After a while it was alright if everybody just minded their own damn business. Her and Devon had even started to get a little side hustle of their own to keep some cash coming in. Monica played a street walker to be the bait for tricks. Meanwhile, Devon would be waiting so he could catch them with their pants down and take them for everything they had. It wasn't anything complicated, but at least they were getting some good money. They had to stay in close contact with each other for the game to work. Sometimes it paid off good and sometimes it didn't, but that's what they would have to do until something better came along. At least Monica didn't have to worry about Devon being in the street pulling armed robberies or running with that treacherous ass Keith Hampton.

Mike Westerling had been watching the clock ever since he came back from lunch. He'd been ready to get the day over with as soon as it started. It was already feeling like the day had been going on forever. He still hadn't dealt with the worst part of it yet. Almost as soon as he walked into the office, he started wishing he could get away from those bright office lights. He hated how everybody's attention in there always seemed to be on him and no one else. Maybe because his name was on the door they thought that made him powerful, but it didn't. The only thing that made him feel powerful was his addiction. The office and his title made him feel like some-body's property. He was sick of the curious stares he caught his co workers giving him. He couldn't wait until he delivered that payoff money. Then he'd have a chance to do what he really wanted to do. He was impatient to get lost in the world he truly loved being in.

He'd been born a Westerling, not some faceless drone. His pedigree meant he wasn't supposed to be like the other work-ers. They were trapped in a system that told them what they had to do. His family were the ones deciding what you were told. He wasn't meant for anonymity, his Westerling bloodline was full of nothing but leaders. The branches coming from his family tree went from big money to major centers of power. The Westerling name had been a force in politics since before the revolutionary war. But he'd been stuck in the Mayor's office for so long he wondered if he was still part of the family. When was he going to get a chance to stand on his own and make a name for himself? Maybe they were afraid of what he could do, that he'd become more than they could handle. They'd never know unless they gave him a chance to shine. The day was coming when he would live up to the promise of his name, and then he was going to make them all sorry that they'd ever doubted him.

As long as he had to take orders from Hector Ortiz and the Italians who owned him, nothing would change. These were the thoughts that kept his mind tangled and turned around. When the day finally ended and he slipped into the luxury seats of his Mercedes Benz sedan, all negative thoughts had to take a break. For a moment he let himself appreciate what a sweet political position he had. All the nice things it allowed him to enjoy was what he deserved. But driving around in a nice car didn't justify them treating him like a delivery boy. He deserved the same respect and authority the rest of his family had. He was tired of having to pay dues and take whatever they threw his way. His name meant he should be enjoying all the benefits of being next in line for the family fortune.

It was after 5:30 pm, almost time to get to the police at the mall in Queens. He had to be on the parking lot roof by 6:30. The cars crawled along in rush hour traffic as his mind wandered back to Sheila and what she did with him. He loved being there with her. He always had the best times with her. Instead of being afraid, she was the queen of his life. He just wanted to please her. He wanted to know that he was who she wanted serving her. He didn't know what was wrong with him. The only joy he felt was when she did what she did to him. There was no better thrill than when he did what she told him to do. There was no other feeling like the one he'd found with her. Before he met her his whole life had been planned out and prepared like a road map. Now that he was under her control, the only place he wanted to be was under her control. The sound of her voice touched him. It was so strong it felt like she had some kind of power over him. When she did things to him it made him feel weak.

That's what he loved about being there. When he was with her he felt secure. With the heroin in him, being high made him accept the things she made him do feel even better. He loved being under her control. It felt good being with her because he knew that was the only place he belonged. When he pulled into the parking ramp and tore off his ticket, he slowly drove past the rows of parked cars. He wondered how long he would have to take orders from criminals. He was better than them, if things didn't change pretty soon he knew he was going to lose his mind. Screeeeech!!! He came out of his daydream just in time to slam on his brakes and stop. He almost ran into the side of that car backing out of a space in front of him. If he would have been paying better attention instead of daydreaming that wouldn't have happened. That's all he needed, to have an accident. That would have been the perfect way to end this day.

The next thing he knew somebody with a pistol was standing next to his window. All he saw was a man in a mask with a gun in their hand. "Roll down the window and don't do nothing stupid." He was too afraid to think, so he did as he was told. If he'd been more like his father, maybe he could have done something to get away. That wouldn't have done him any good, the car he almost hit was still in front of him. The guy reached in the window and opened the door. "Put it in park, give me your phone, and get out." Westerling was shaking like a leaf, he started feeling light headed like he was going to faint. The gunman snatched the keys and pulled him out of the car. He yanked the frightened man to the back of the car and opened up the trunk. He took the briefcase out and pushed Westerling in. "Alright get your ass in there, and you better not make a sound. If I hear any noise back here I'm going to fill the back seat up with bullets." Westerling fearfully nodded his head and made room for himself in the trunk. He was moving so slow the gunman pushed him in and slammed the lid down. The robber got behind the wheel, and signaled the car in front to pull off. All they had to do was get out of the area as fast as they could.

The Mercedes followed the other car around the ramp and drove out the same way they'd come in. Everything had gone down smooth but it wasn't time to celebrate. When they were out of the parking ramp they pulled off their stocking masks. After driving a few blocks away, there was a nice quiet residential street to park on. When the first car pulled over the Mercedes stopped a little ways down the street. Before he got out, the robber told his captive passenger, "Listen, I'm going to hit the trunk release and let you out, but if I was you I'd stay in there about five more minutes. I'll be waiting down the street to see if you know how to follow instructions. I wouldn't advise you to get out before I leave. Don't be a fool unless you feel like dying today." He got out of the Mercedes with the brief case and got into the other car. They were nervous but excited, the hard part was done.

All they had to do now was get back home. They still couldn't feel too happy. Once they got on the highway, and were far away from where they'd done the robbery, they laughed and let off the tension with yells of triumph. That was all they could do to celebrate their success. They couldn't stop smiling when they saw what was inside the briefcase. There were rows of fifty and one hundred dollar bills stacked side by side on top of each other. The next move was to get that car back to the Bronx. The crackhead that pawned it to them didn't have a clue about what they'd done. Since Alphonso was driving, there was no way the car could get traced back to them. When they got back to the Bronx, Alphonso pulled up next to Mike's black Escalade. Mike got out with the briefcase and pulled out of the parking space. Alphonso parked the bucket where Mike's truck had been. They were all smiles with the briefcase sitting right between them.

On the way back to the building Alphonso asked, "What now? What are we doing with all this money?" Mike had already planned for that before they ever went to the parking ramp. "First we have to count it and know what the split is, then we'll stash it until we figure out what we're going to do next." He looked at Alphonso and said, "Do you want your cut now or do you want to wait until things calm down?" Mike already knew there wouldn't be any noise about the robbery, and there was no way anybody could know what they'd done. Everything had gone so smooth it had been like an early Christmas present. Each of the stacks was $5,000 and there were 30 of them inside the case. Mike had to split his half with Alphonso because Sheila and him had agreed to split it down the middle. Since he'd only drove and didn't have to do anything else Alphonso took $25,000 for his cut. That left Mike with $50,000 for his share. Alphonso was the naturally cautious type so he wasn't going to do anything that could attract attention. He wasn't broke and wasn't trying to do anything big. "Yo man, you can just hold onto mine until you're ready to make a move with yours. If you want to do something slick maybe I'll get down on it with you. Just make sure you put it somewhere that can't nobody touch it." Mike almost broke his face smirking. "Man ain't nobody but me and you going to know where this dough is or what they've got to do to touch it. Just make sure you don't let none of them bitches you be running with clip your ass for it." He laughed at the face Alphonso made when they drove to the back of the building.

Westerling waited those five minutes and then a little longer before he cautiously climbed out of the trunk. The first thing he did when he got back in the car was look at his face in the mirror. He wanted to see the size of the lump he could feel growing on the side of his head. He shouldn't have been worried about that as much as what he was going to tell Ortiz and the goons he worked for. All they'd want to know was how he'd gotten robbed. None of them cared how afraid he'd been or how big the gun was that was pointed in his face. They'd probably laugh when he told them he just didn't want to get shot. All they cared about was the money. They'll worry about punishing whoever took it later. The more he thought about what he had to go through, the more he panicked.

Westerling stopped thinking and started the car, he needed to get somewhere he could think by himself. He had to get his mind together, and out of instinct he headed for the safety of his office. He knew he would have to do something, but he didn't know what it was going to be. After what he'd been through, what would make him feel better was a drink. It was almost 7:00 pm. The traffic around city hall was thinning out. He parked around the corner from the park and slipped in the employees entrance at the back of the building. Once inside he headed straight for his office and rushed over to his desk.

In the bottom drawer was a bottle of Patron. He'd hidden it in there just in case he ever had to have one. This definitely qualified as one of those times. He collapsed into his chair and grabbed one of the crystal water glasses off his desk. He poured himself a generous drink, at this point he didn't think anything mattered. He poured the liquid fire down his throat and welcomed the burn of its entrance. The painful trail scorched a path to his empty stomach that brought tears to his eyes. He put his elbows on his desk and held his head in his hands. He stayed like that until he needed another drink.

The only thing he could focus on was how hard it was going to be to explain to Ortiz what happened to his money. That's when he really got scared. What if Ortiz and his goons thought he had something to do with it? The more he thought about that, the more desperate he became. How could he explain getting robbed? Would they even believe him when he said he didn't have any choice? The more he thought about how they'd react, the more hopeless he felt. He'd been drinking for more than an hour, but the liquor still hadn't calmed him down. He felt drunk, but not drunk enough to try and face Ortiz. He picked up the keys laying on his desk and put the smallest one in the largest desk drawer. He opened it and took out a brown, suede covered case.

There was something inside it he never thought he'd need. He flipped the case open and stared at what was inside. The sinister shine coming from the 38 automatic pistol was almost hypnotizing. The swirling white pearl handle and chrome finish gave it an attractive yet threatening appearance. He'd never liked the silver chrome plating or mother of pearl handle, but he still had to admit it was a pretty gun. It had been a gift from Hector Ortiz. He gave it to him after he was appointed to the Mayor's Community Response Team. Now it might be the only way out of the mess he was in. If he pulled the trigger with it in his mouth all of his problems would be over. Nobody would have to know why he did it. It was better than letting his family down. By now the mob and police had all of their people on high alert. They were looking for his car everywhere, trying to find him or figure out where he'd gone. Since they hadn't seen him or heard from him by now they probably figured he'd ripped them off.

Westerling still didn't have the nerve to go outside. He clung to the security of his darkened office and kept drinking, trying to come up with a story that wouldn't lay all the blame on him for the missing money. He wasn't drunk enough or brave enough to leave his office until it was after 11 o clock. He didn't have anywhere else he could go and be safe so he went to see if Sheila could help him. The darkness and the booze gave him enough courage to drive to the club. He knew she wasn't going to want to see him looking like that, but he didn't care anymore. He was dirty and stained from being in the trunk, and he smelled bad from sitting in his office getting drunk. His clothes were all sweaty and his face looked dirty. He hadn't shaved since he went to work that morning, so his shadow was out of control. What he really looked was panicked and afraid. When he got to the afterhours club his odor got to the door before he did. The bouncer knew who he was so he let him pass, but when he walked up to the bar it was a different story. "Hi Freda, can I please see Sheila?" She tried not to react to the smell but she couldn't keep her face from reacting. "I'll call her down for you Mike, can I get you anything to drink?" It was something she asked out of habit, he already smelled like a bottle. "Yes please, let me have a double shot of Patron." Freda nodded and left happily because the liquor was all the way at the other end of the bar.

While Freda was making his drink she got on the phone and called for Layla to come downstairs. When Layla got to the bar she told her, "Girl check Mike out over there, he looks like he's been put through a wringer. He said he wants to see Sheila. I called you down here to make the call on that. I'll tell you one thing, he smells like he just fell off a shit truck. I'm letting myself out of this one here." In a sarcastic tone Layla told her, "Thanks so much for all your help, I'll handle him." She went over to where he was sitting and in spite of the pungent aroma said, "Hello Mike, is there anything I can do for you?" He looked up without letting go of his drink and said, "Hi Layla, all I need to do is talk to Sheila. I really need her to let me know something. It's very important."

Layla didn't know what she was supposed to make of that so she said, "I'm sorry but Sheila's working right now. Unless you're here to take care of some kind of business with her I can't let her come down." He hurriedly said, "Can't I just get her to talk to me?" Layla wasn't letting him get any further with his story than that. "Mike, I don't think you understand, Sheila gets paid to work not talk, if you want to talk to her you'll have to talk to her when you're paying to see her." Westerling didn't care about that he was ready to do whatever he had to do. "I'll pay her if that's what I have to do. I just want to have some time with Sheila tonight. I'll pay the $200 if I can still go upstairs. Can I see her now?" Layla wasn't going to stop him from paying so she said, "Sure you can see her Mike, as soon as she's free I'll send her down to get you." "Alright Layla, I'll be right here."

Layla went back upstairs and told Sheila what she had on

her menu, "Girl, your favorite date is downstairs, and he's waiting for the one and only you again." Sheila knew who she was talking about, but rolled her eyes and said, "I don't know what I'm supposed to do for him. He ain't no good to nobody once he gets that dope in him. His joint don't even raise up after he gets high." Layla just shook her head and said, "As long as he pays the $200 you'll have to do the best you can. I know one thing, tonight you're really going to earn your cut. He smells like he fell off a garbage truck." Sheila turned up her lip and said, "Well if he wants me to do anything with his ass he's going to have to take a shower. He pays good money to get slapped around and talked to a little rough, he'll be clean before I do any of that tonight. I won't touch his dirty ass if he stinks." Layla just shook her head, she didn't need to hear any of their gory details. What they did stayed between them. "I was just trying to let you know what you were up against. Since he said he only wants you, whatever you do with him you're going to make $75. No matter what, make sure he knows all he gets is one hour." Sheila shrugged her shoulders on her way to the bar.

As soon as Westerling saw Sheila, he got off the bar stool and rushed over to her. The smell hit her nose before she was ready for it. She retreated back and sternly said, "Mike, come upstairs with me." "Yes Miss Sheila I'll do whatever you want." "Follow me up the stairs, and don't stay too far back. If you do I'll punish you." He followed her and immediately began assuming a meek and submissive attitude. Once they were in the room, in a very authoritative voice she said, "Mike, you smell foul don't you? You smell like you need a bath, are you clean?" Westerling bowed his head and whispered, "No Miss Sheila, I'm sorry. I know I'm not clean, I've been through a very hard day today." Sheila's voice took on the disciplined tone of a drill sergeant, "I don't care what kind of day you had, I told you before that you're never supposed to come to me smelling like this. If you ever try this again you'll be punished in the worst way. Now take off your clothes and get in the shower right now. I won't waste my time with you until you're clean. You're not allowed in my presence until you show me the proper respect. I've told you before to keep yourself clean haven't I? Do you want to be whipped for your disobedience?" "No Miss Sheila I'll do anything you tell me to do."

He stripped off his clothes whining about how he wanted to talk to her. "I just want you to know how sorry I am for what I've done. I don't want to do bad things but I have to do what they tell me. If I don't obey them they'll hurt me or my family." Sheila heard him and gave him exactly what he needed. "You will always obey me, and always do what Miss Sheila commands." "Yes I will obey you Miss Sheila." She couldn't stand the sight or smell of him anymore. "Now go get in the shower. I'll listen to you after you're clean. That's when you can tell me what you want me to know." Twenty minutes later, Westerling came out of the shower naked, with a towel around his waist. Sheila said, "You came to me dirty. Now I'm going to show you what I'll do to you if you ever do it again. Turn around and let go of the towel."

He turned around and dropped the towel. Then she swung her cat of nine tails across his exposed behind. Smack! He flinched from the pain and shock of the lashes, but didn't cover his ass or try to escape. Again and again she struck him with the whip, each one harder than before. She was trying to make him react to the pain or at least move away, but he just accepted all of it. The welts on his behind were beginning to swell and turn an angry red. When she saw how raw it looked she stopped. In her sternest tone of voice she said, "That's what you deserve when you disrespect me. Now don't ever come here unprepared to see me. Now turn around so I can find out if you're ready to be a good slave." When he turned back around she could see that his dick was stiff. The whipping had been enough to excite him. The whip made him want more of the same treatment. That's why he came to her, he came there for what she gave him. He wanted her to be happy, so he held his hard dick and stroked it. He was proud of himself for keeping his dick hard for her.

Sheila wanted to know why he was there so early, and why he was in such bad shape. She couldn't just ask him so she said, "I'll always treat you like you deserve to be treated. But you have to prove to me you're the kind of slave I've trained you to be. Now why did you come here looking for me tonight?" "Miss Sheila, I came because I'm in trouble. I need your help because I don't know what to do. I need you to protect me from the bad men I told you about. They're looking for me because they think I stole their money. But I didn't steal it Miss Sheila, somebody else did. But I can't tell them that, they'll never believe me."

She wanted to hear about the money, but first she had to find out how she could make things better for her. "Tell me what happened, and don't leave anything out. I'll decide if I can help you or not when I know what happened. If you don't do what I tell you to do, you'll have to figure it out for yourself." Without any hesitation Westerling told her about what happened, he even told her about the pistol he had in his car. What he didn't bother to mention were his suicidal thoughts or anything about the depression and desperation he felt. He didn't want her to know how sad he was or how worried he was about where his life was headed. He needed her to point him in the right direction and give him something to hope for. "Miss Sheila I don't know what they're going to do to me. Please, can't you just tell me what I need to do?"

Sheila cared about doing what she had to do to keep suspicion from coming back to her. She had to build up his nerve enough so that he would think he could face the music on his own. "Alright now listen to me Mike, if you didn't do anything wrong you don't have anything to be afraid of. I'm going to tell you what to do, and you're going to have to do exactly what I say. Can you follow my directions?" "Yes Miss Sheila, I will obey you." When she was sure he was under her control and dependent on her she said, "You haven't done anything wrong. You did exactly what they said and something bad still happened to you. You didn't do anything bad, something bad happened to you. It wasn't your fault was it?" Westerling was shaking but he knew what he had to say. "No Miss Sheila, it wasn't my fault, I was doing exactly what they told me to do." Sheila told him, "Since all you did was follow their instructions, I'm going to make sure you're protected. You have to obey me and do what I tell you to do. I'm going to say some incantations and cast a special spell that will control what happens in your life. As long as you obey me and stay under my protection you'll be safe. I want you to stay inside the club for a few more hours and let them wonder where you are. When you show back up they'll be relieved you're back. They'll listen to what you say and they'll believe everything you tell them about what happened".

Sheila had spent more time with him than she wanted, but she had found out everything she needed to know. Mike had done what he said he was going to do. Now her job was to make sure Westerling didn't say or do anything that would bring any suspicion back to her or the club. When his erection was gone she was finished with him. Sheila got him back dressed and looking presentable enough to go back out in the bar. Before he left she told him, "Alright listen, you have to do everything I tell you. I'm not going to let you come back until you've done what I want." Westerling listened to her every word. It was like he'd been transformed into a small child when she spoke. All he needed was a few harsh words and some painful slaps to fulfill his fantasy. She could get him to do whatever she wanted with just a little more of her rough attention. "Miss Sheila, can you let me see you on the outside? I know I can't come here but can you meet me somewhere else just for a little while?"

Sheila wasn't going to negotiate with him, but if he wanted to hear that so he could do what he had to do she figured why not. "You have to obey me before anything else. I won't give you any special treatment unless you're obedient. Do as I tell you and then I'll decide what I want to do for you." He wasn't happy about it but he knew better than to say anything. "I promise you I'll obey you Miss Sheila. I'm a good slave and I'll make you proud of me." Sheila said, "Just make sure you stay inside the bar until you're sober enough to keep your story straight. If they don't believe you there's nothing I can do to protect you. When you tell them what happened, if they say you aren't telling them the truth remind them of your loyalty and how much you fear their power." Westerling listened intently, he wasn't going to forget a single word she said. "Now go back downstairs and drink coffee until you're sober enough to drive." It was after 2:00 am when he finally left the bar. He knew where he was supposed to go, but he was afraid.

He still wasn't brave enough to face them. He felt like he was stuck, he couldn't go back to Sheila, and he was too afraid to go to Ortiz. Blindly he drove around the city thinking about what he had to do. He never stopped blaming himself for everything that had gone wrong in his life.

www.ingramcontent.com/pod-product-compliance
Lightning Source LLC
Chambersburg PA
CBHW051233130726

47988CB00001B/330